THE SHAPE OF BONES

Daniel Galera

Translated by ALISON ENTREKIN

HAMISH HAMILTON
an imprint of
PENGUIN BOOKS

HAMISH HAMILTON

UK | USA | Canada | Ireland | Australia
India | New Zealand | South Africa

Hamish Hamilton is part of the Penguin Random House group of companies
whose addresses can be found at global.penguinrandomhouse.com

First published as *Mãos de Cavalo* in Brazil by Companhia das Letras 2006
This translation first published in Great Britain by Hamish Hamilton 2017

001

Copyright © Daniel Galera, 2006, 2017
Translation copyright © Alison Entrekin, 2017

The moral right of the author has been asserted

Set in 14/17 pt Fournier MT Std
Typeset by Jouve (UK), Milton Keynes
Printed in Great Britain by Clays Ltd, St Ives plc

A CIP catalogue record for this book is available from the British Library

HARDBACK ISBN: 978–0–241–14594–4

www.greenpenguin.co.uk

MIX
Paper from
responsible sources
FSC
www.fsc.org   FSC® C018179

Penguin Random House is committed to a
sustainable future for our business, our readers
and our planet. This book is made from Forest
Stewardship Council® certified paper.

For my parents and brother

I would walk to school and actually have crane shots worked out in my mind where the crane would be pulling up and looking down at me as a tiny object in the street walking to school.

Nicolas Cage

THE SHAPE OF BONES

By the same author

Blood-Drenched Beard

THE URBAN CYCLIST

No terrain is impossible for the Urban Cyclist. His powerful legs drive the pedals down in alternation, right, left, right, left, calculating the degree of incline by the strength required of his thigh and calf muscles for each complete revolution of the front sprocket. The soles of his feet and palms of his hands read each vibration transferred from the tyres to the handlebars and frame, making micro-adjustments to his direction and balance at a speed faster than thought. The initial uphill stretch when he first leaves the house is short and serves to lubri-cate his joints and warm up his muscles. He quickly reaches Reservation Street. Its sloping cobbled lanes are separated by a grassy central reservation. Five blocks to The Strip. Knowing every inch of the way like the back of his hand doesn't make the challenge any less dangerous for the Urban Cyclist. From one week to the next, so much can change. A resident might decide to have a new driveway put in so they can park their car in the garage more comfortably, and may have to deposit mounds of sand, gravel and cement in the middle of the pavement, an example of the kind of mutant obstacle for which the true Urban Cyclist must be prepared. There are dogs that shoot out like rockets from behind walls to try to snaffle a bit of their favourite food, an unwary cyclist's shin. Even trees, an apparently peaceful and inoffensive element of the natural world, from one week to the next push out branches and roots, which can obstruct the Cyclist's path. Weeds sprout from the pavement, concealing pebbles, holes and bricks that can catch one by surprise and cause serious accidents from which only the most skilled, experienced cyclists emerge unscathed.

The day is auspicious for a high-risk, high-speed ride. It's chilly out, with a cold wind of medium intensity and a clear sky. Although the wind causes certain discomfort, whipping the Cyclist's face and making breathing difficult, it means he perspires less, thus reducing the need to wipe sweat from his eyes and the risk of his hand slipping on the bike's plastic grips, an accident whose price would be nothing less than a few broken teeth and ribs.

On Reservation Street, he slows almost to a complete halt and gazes for a few seconds at the five-block slope stretching down before him like the throat of a giant pachyderm. Balancing like this without touching the ground requires excellent technique from the rider and perfect synchronicity between cyclist and bike, a synchronicity which the Urban Cyclist most definitely shares with his old-fashioned-but-fierce, white-framed, blue-stickered 20" Caloi Cross BMX, with a foot brake and red balloon tyres with a grooved tread in the place of the slim black originals, which were unsuited to the speed and terrain of elite urban cycling.

After a few seconds analysing his course, which includes checking for traffic coming up or down the street, pedestrians or animals on the pavement, moisture in the terrain, the thrust of the wind and the chance of rain, among other things, and already confident, after careful inspection back in his garage, that the bike is in a perfect state of maintenance, including wheel alignment, spoke adjustment, brake function and air pressure in tyres, as well as chain, bearing and sprocket lubrication (a few drops of Singer oil on the main articulated parts are essential), the Urban Cyclist launches himself downhill, pedalling at such a breakneck speed that any observer would be dumbfounded.

With a few quick turns of the pedals, he attains a speed at which the vibration of the wheels on the cobblestones is almost too much to bear. But the Cyclist is familiar with this stretch and knows he must hold his wrists firm for a few more seconds until, with a sharp manoeuvre to the left that would seem like madness to your average cyclist, he jumps over the central reservation, taking advantage of a kerb cut, crosses the oncoming lane, shoots diagonally up a driveway to the pavement and deftly executes a quick right-hand swerve with the handlebars just in time to avoid colliding head-on with an unfinished cement wall whose surface looks as though bits of human skin and flesh would adhere to it nicely. This is the first of five tricky spots in today's course, assuming, that is, that there are no surprises. Now on the pavement, the Cyclist passes five houses without many bumps or changes in the terrain, and allows himself to relax for a few seconds, reposition his hands on the grips, release the tension in his knees and elbows, and quickly take in the view until his gaze finds the waters of the Guaíba in the distance, dotted with white sails. On his right, now, are houses built within the last year, several with still-immaculate paint and roof tiles, separated from one another by mini-forests. On his left, the land is predominantly arid with long eroded strips of hard, orange dirt that extend down to the foot of the hill and give way to a flat area where extremely straight streets demarcate rectangular blocks divided into plots of land for sale. The subdivision of Porto Alegre's southern suburbs is new, and few, to date, have taken up residence there. The Cyclist is a pioneer intent on

4

mapping every inch of this inhospitable zone with his fearless wheels. An intersection. His ears quickly sweep the surroundings for noises that might indicate the potential threat of motor vehicles. Negative. Only the repetitive chirping of birds. A jump from kerb to street, vibration. He returns to the kerb with a wheelie, swerves around the stump of a sawn-off tree that is still oozing bubbly resin and comes to the second tricky spot, a sequence of three adjacent driveways whose ramps form a series of stairs. The Cyclist pedals backwards, applying light pressure to the brakes, vaulting from one level to the next at precisely the right speed. Jump, jump, jump. Sweat is already streaming in salty beads from his temples and pooling above his upper lip. The sandstone pavement suddenly disappears and gives way to a patch of brush that conceals a tangle of tree roots. This is the third tricky spot, perhaps the most dangerous of all, because the roots are hidden and no matter how many times he's ridden it it's impossible to memorize them all. Here the Urban Cyclist recognizes that his planning counts for nothing. The terrain calls the shots and decides if you are going to fall or not; all he can do is steady his wrists and be careful to relax his arm and leg joints so that they can act as natural shock-absorbers, leaving enough slack for the bike to transfer the impact to his muscles. The most important thing is for rider and bike to maintain their balance as they cross the grass studded with traps of live wood, which may also contain a cruel shard of glass, a rusty tin can or a dead opossum. When he gets to the end of the pavement, everything is still under control. He jumps over the kerb again but doesn't return to the pavement, as he knows he will soon come to a long stretch of dense vegetation that is impossible to cross. An elite urban cyclist must above all master the art of simultaneously dividing his attention between the front wheel of his bike, the terrain directly in front of him, and whatever is coming up a few dozen yards off. To neglect to do so can be costly when traversing such wild, unpredictable terrain as this at such a high speed. He knew in advance, thanks to his powers of observation, that he wouldn't return to the pavement at this point, and he continues down the middle of the street, bracing himself through a new stretch of intense vibration on the cobblestones until he reaches the end of Reservation Street and the fourth tricky spot, The Strip.

The Strip is a tarmacked avenue. His course only takes in fifty-odd yards of it, until he can take a right on Shade Street and follow it to his final objective, Guaíba Avenue. To an urban cyclist, fifty yards of docile, smooth tarmac should be a breeze. But when this stretch of tarmac has cars, buses, trucks and carts travelling along it in both directions, and you arrive at it from a perpendicular cobbled street at something like twenty-five miles an hour, or thirty-six feet a second, it becomes tricky spot number four. The Urban Cyclist requires a very light, stripped-back bike, like his 20" Caloi with the foot brake, for situations like this. He doesn't wear a helmet, gloves, toe clips, or Lycra shorts that cling to his rear. That's for girls. The Urban Cyclist wears ordinary trainers, shorts that allow plenty of air circulation, a short-sleeved T-shirt in summer and a long-sleeved one in winter. That's it. A cap is allowed on rainy days or when it's very sunny. As for the foot brake, the Cyclist knows it is scoffed at by most cyclists, who consider it old-fashioned, unsafe and hard to operate. It does take a great deal of training to really master the foot brake, it is true, but once you have the hang of it, you'll never want to change to a modern braking system, with levers on the handlebars. The Urban Cyclist jams on his trusty foot brake with a backward turn of the pedal and goes into a skid across the cobblestones. The fine layer of sand and gravel covering the last few yards of the street influences the bike's behaviour, reducing its traction to a negligible level. This has, of course, been taken into account by the Cyclist, who carries out a visual survey of the traffic on both lanes of The Strip and decides that he doesn't need to brake fully. On the contrary, he skilfully accelerates out of the skid and crosses The Strip, watched by two women at a bus stop, who are shocked at his audacity. There isn't time to show off. He picks up speed on the tarmac, eighteen, nineteen, twenty feet a second, and now makes a wide curve to the right, perfect and safe. Shade Street is even bumpier than Reservation Street. He has no choice but to take one of the pavements. The one on the right offers the most exciting ride. Although deeply focused, the Urban Cyclist savours his secret: the pavements of residential streets in big cities. Nobody else recognizes them as the ultimate terrain for the practice of high-level radical stunt riding. He makes an S around two trees in close sequence, swerving first right, then left. In the foreground is the sound of his tyres on the different kinds of pavement, the wind in his ears, the metallic taste of speed. Only he knows this pleasure. He crosses another street and returns to the pavement of the next block. He can see Guaíba Avenue, skirting the vast expanse of brown water. This is the home stretch.

The bike becomes airborne. He has made a mistake. He forgot the fifth tricky spot: the slimy pavement, a permanently moist section beneath a roof of treetops that does justice to the nickname

'Shade Street' and is always covered in slime. Almost zero traction. Slippery as soap. The bike went into a skid and he thought about throwing himself to the ground, but there wasn't time, because the front wheel hit the low retaining wall of a tiny flowerbed graced with a dozen pansies and camellias, and now he and the bike are sailing through the air, and now they are tumbling over the cobblestones of Shade Street, the Cyclist's foot caught in the frame of his 20" Caloi with the foot brake, and they roll and slide together for several yards, leaving a wake of dust behind them.

The Urban Cyclist lies in the middle of the street for at least ten seconds, his leg still caught in the bike, while the neighbourhood dogs bark in a frenzy. When his brain starts working again, the first thing that occurs to him is that his face must be deformed. He runs his hand over it and finds a little blood on his thumb. His tongue registers the sour taste and what appears to be a small flap of loose skin on his lower lip. He frees his leg from the bike, the right one, and examines it. A small white circle under his knee begins to sprout minuscule red dots, which become drops of blood that swell and start to run down his leg. Parts of his body that were numb begin to sting. A tickle in his nose, a knot in his throat, and he can't hold back the tears. They aren't tears of pain or of fear, really, although he is afraid, afraid of his face being deformed, of having to have stitches at the emergency room, of lots of things, but he cries above all out of frustration. Just as mountains can grow angry and greet the most able and respected climber with an avalanche, this time the pavement has greeted him with a surface of slimy stones and he has been brought down by his opponent in a moment of distraction, a stupid moment of distraction. He has fallen.

He is no longer the Urban Cyclist. Now he is just a ten-year-old boy. But the street is quiet, there are no cars or people around. It is almost three o'clock on a Wednesday afternoon and everyone is busy with something, no one is out and about, much less on a remote residential street in the southern suburbs where people don't have much reason to leave their houses except to go to work or to run errands downtown. He decides to get up and go and look for help, maybe call home from a public phone and reverse the charge. He has no difficulty standing up. He wipes the blood from his mouth again. He wishes he had a mirror now – more than anything, a mirror. He walks towards Guaíba Avenue, where there are bars and a phone booth and people jogging. He is fine until he glances down at his knee. Through the wound – a hole half an inch in diameter and of considerable depth for a surface as devoid of padding as a knee – the blood now runs freely down his shin, drenching his white cotton socks. Something isn't right. His legs feel weak and his entire body is covered with a fine sweat, very different from the sweat worked up previously through physical effort.

He looks for something to lean on, but can't find anything. The dizziness is too much. He falls to the ground, on the pavement. And what he sees beside him, crouching there, is a kitten. A mottled grey kitten tied with a length of blue string to a barbed-wire fence. The improvised collar is no more than six inches long. The kitten looks weak but, feeling threatened, it meows and shows its teeth. Woozy, the Cyclist lifts his head and sees a little old lady closing a wooden gate and walking towards him. Perhaps influenced by the kitten, his first reaction is fear, but then he realizes that the old lady is his salvation, help. She leans over to console him.

'That was quite a tumble, child. Don't cry, don't cry, let me see.'

Her voice is a little hoarse, but at the same time sweet and contrived like that of a children's TV show hostess. Her hair is light brown, her face is criss-crossed with fine, shallow wrinkles, and she has no neck. Her head looks as if it has been screwed straight on to her body. She is wearing a long skirt, which must have been red and is now a faded pink, and a light-beige jumper.

'Give Grandma a look. It's nothing.'

After the good first impression, he begins to find her a little menacing and isn't sure if he should trust her. The kitten is huddled against the barbed wire. The woman leans over. He notices she is missing two fingers from one hand. The little finger and the one next to it. The pinkie and the ring finger.

'I think you bit your lip when you fell, child. It'll be better in no time. It's nothing. No need to cry.'

Being treated like a child adds a pinch of resentment to his feelings of misgiving. No one should ever be treated like a child, not even a child. And he isn't even crying any more.

Then she sees his knee, and the blood that has now run down his shin and is dripping on to the ground. She studies the wound for a moment and seems undecided as to what to do. He wants her to leave, hurry off and find someone with a car who can take him home. Or go back to wherever she came from, so that he can get up and race away in any direction, even though he is dizzy and injured. The kitten meows repeatedly, and only now does it occur to him that there is something very wrong about a kitten being tied so cruelly to a barbed-wire fence. There is only vegetation on the other side, but it was from there, from that plot of land, that the old lady appeared. Through gaps in the grass, he makes out parts of what appears to be a wooden shack patched together with sheets of plywood.

He toys half-seriously with the thought that she might be a witch. If it's true, she's a good actress. Her expression is benevolent and maternal.

'That blood there, you know, that's bad blood.'

He looks at her with bulging, quizzical eyes.

'You know there's good blood and bad blood, don't you? Bad blood is that dark blood coming out there, it's dirty blood. It runs just under the surface, like this, near the skin, see?' she says, showing him her own arm and running the tip of her index finger over her wrinkled brown skin. 'Good blood is different, it's lighter in colour, almost pink, and it runs through the big veins, deep inside, through your flesh.' He notes that her drawl is from the interior. 'That bad blood there, it's good that it's coming out. You've got to let it out, because then your body will make more of the good blood, the clean sort that runs through the inside, to replace the bad blood, understand?'

The woman pats his head and smiles. He looks at his knee again and sees that the blood really is dark. He tries to imagine the colour of the good blood, so clean it's almost pink. He has never seen this kind of blood, or at least he can't remember having seen it. Maybe the blood he bled when his baby molars fell out. He remembers that when he spat, the blood was pretty light in colour. But the blood oozing out now is definitely bad blood, full of impurities, as if it were dirty with coal soot, drawing lines across his almost hairless shin.

The more he thinks about it, the less queasy he feels about his injuries. He imagines an elaborate picture of every vein and artery running through him like a drain network, but made of muscle, soft flesh supported and articulated by bones. He swipes the blood on his leg with his index finger and then presses it to his thumb, feeling them stick together. He has stopped sweating and doesn't feel dizzy any more. On the contrary, his energy is returning. His aches and pains are worse, but now he bears them with a certain pleasure. He stands, brushes himself off, finds several minor scratches on his elbows and shoulders and goes to see how his bike has fared. The chain has come off, but he slots it back on to the sprockets, dirtying his fingers with the dark goo that is a mixture of lube and dust, and gives the pedal a quick half spin. With a click, the links of the chain re-engage with the metal teeth. The old lady offers a few last words of comfort. Without answering, he climbs on his bike and begins to pedal home. The true Urban Cyclist cannot be fazed by wounds and bleeding resulting from the accidents that sooner or later happen. His knee continues to bleed all the way back up Reservation Street, shedding bad blood. A trickle of red runs from his lower lip over his chin and drips between his legs from time to time. It is as if cameras hidden behind lamp posts are recording his physical tenacity, his dynamic recovery after a spectacular fall. Every red drop is awaited with anticipation.

6.08 A.M.

Firmly gripping the steering wheel of the car he was about to drive for four days and three nights to the highest part of the Bolivian Plateau, he felt the queasiness typical of that last moment in which it still seems possible to turn your back on something, although, deep down, you know you can't because it was all decided and planned a long time ago. This useless hesitation was made even more uncomfortable by the pervasive six o'clock silence of this Saturday morning. Instead of turning the key in the ignition, he sat waiting for a sound, as if it might provide the finger-flick needed to propel him forward, make him start the car, drive to Renan's place to pick him up at the agreed time, and set out on what promised to be the biggest adventure of his life. Adri had informed him the night before that she wouldn't be getting up to see him off. So, from the moment the alarm on his mobile phone had begun to play *The Addams Family* theme song at 5.15 a.m., he had made as much noise as possible, peeing, washing his face, pulling on a pair of comfortable tracksuit bottoms, a polo shirt, running shoes and a cap with the clinic's logo on it, fixing himself a bowl of full-fat yogurt with granola and a ridiculous amount of honey, brushing his teeth, deliberately bumping into the bed and the stool in the walk-in wardrobe, tuning into an AM radio station for the weather forecast at an unnecessarily high volume, wandering back into the master bedroom and quickly leaving again, opening Nara's bedroom door, almost disturbing her toddler sleep in the hope that it might soften his wife's heart, opening and closing the car boot to peer at the bags he had packed, organized and checked a zillion times the night before, going back inside for no reason and, finally, leaving, closing the garage for the last time and angrily slamming the car door. But despite his efforts, Adri had kept her promise. She was probably still pretending to be asleep, waiting for the brief electric squeal of the ignition to start the combustion cycles of the pistons in the Mitsubishi Montero. He finally decided to give her the satisfaction and turned the key, revving a few times in neutral for the pleasure of breaking the silence, fantasizing that at that very moment, lying in bed, realizing that he really was going, she was feeling mortally sorry that she hadn't given him a goodbye kiss, even if only on the cheek, and wished him good luck. Backing the car slowly down the parallel strips of granite that ran across the neat front lawn, he decided to turn off his mobile as soon as he hit the highway and wait two or three days before calling to check in. With the city streets deserted, he hoped to make it to Renan's property in Vila Nova in twenty-five minutes at the most. He kept the car windows closed, and the noise of the tyres on the irregular paving stones sounded faraway and soft, making him feel as if he were inside an aquarium, cut off from the world. He opened the driver's window all the way and everything transformed, starting with the crunching sound of the tyres. The sun, no doubt rising behind a building, cast a hazy pinkish-yellow light over the houses, buildings, trees and cobblestones of Bela Vista's side streets. The heroic stars lingered in the sky, which had ceased to be nocturnal about five, maximum ten, minutes earlier. The air was cool and saturated with oxygen. He drew it into his lungs through his nose, filling his alveoli to the brim, and held his breath for a few seconds. In a few days he and Renan would be 13,420 feet above sea level in a guesthouse in Potosí, which shared the title of the highest city on the planet with Lhasa, in Tibet, lying on bunk beds, resting up and ingesting large volumes of liquid until they were properly acclimatized, trying not to ruin everything at the outset with a pulmonary embolism. When he turned on to Carlos Trein Filho Street, which would take him to Nilo Peçanha Avenue, he remembered the question that Renan had asked out of the blue as they rested on the top of Cruz Rock, late on a Sunday afternoon in April, almost seven months earlier. They had just climbed the 'Via Prosciutto Crudo', as Renan had christened it. After a two-week climbing vacation in Sardinia, in August 2002, Renan had started giving his climbs random names in Italian. That was probably the best weekend they had spent in Minas do Camaquã, a ghostly village near a set of rocky formations that looked like a sequence of four giant waves of solid rock pushing up out of a landscape of rolling hills and rivers. Situated in Brazil's deep south, the village dated back to the early twentieth century, when copper, gold and silver were discovered in the region. Mining had ceased when the reserves were depleted in the mid 1990s. The village was now inhabited by one or two hundred families, mostly retired miners, and its abandoned houses and streets, set in a landscape mutilated by mining, gave a charming end-of-the-world atmosphere to a place that was already naturally isolated. He, Renan and a small group of fellow gym members were among the first climbers to start visiting the region. They'd travel the 185 miles from Porto Alegre to Minas do Camaquã early on the Saturday morning, spend the day climbing and the night barbecuing, climb a little more on the Sunday, and return that night, Renan to the indoor climbing walls of Condor, the gym he owned, and he to his practice and the operating rooms of Mãe de Deus Hospital. To him, climbing had always been a way to test his physical and mental limits, an enjoyable exercise in muscular resistance and concentration, practised with discipline and regularity. It had become an integral part of his daily life, but when he managed to take a break from his patients and join the group from Condor for a weekend outing, it became something more, a set of parentheses in the more or less predictable flow of his professional and family life. To Renan, on the other hand, climbing was his routine. When he wasn't working as instructor and managing partner at Condor or teaching rock climbing to private groups and institutions, he was somewhere in Brazil, Latin America or the world, on climbs with difficulty ratings of 9 or 10 on the Brazilian scale, amassing gigabytes in digital photographs to record his considerable climbing feats, like when he free-climbed the Massa Crítica, in Rio, in record time, and what he called the 'Francobolo', currently considered the most difficult route in Brazil's south, a 10b climb that involved walking across the ceiling of Terceira Légua Cave,

in Caxias do Sul, with explosive-sounding footsteps. Although the relationship between their egos
and climbing was somewhat different, he and
Renan had been fast friends ever since they'd met
at Condor, and whenever their agendas coincided
they'd go away for weekend climbs, on an average
of ten times a year over the last three years. They'd
been to Itacolomi, Torres, Cotiporã, Salto Ventoso,
Pico da Canastra and Ivoti. But their favourite destination was Minas do Camaquã, where camping
on the Saturday night was so much fun, with bon-
fires and conversations that stretched into the night,
that on one occasion he'd convinced Adri to leave
Nara with his parents and go with him, despite the
fear she felt when she saw other human beings dangling from great heights, a fear he had jokingly
defined as 'vicarious acrophobia', which Renan had
described as 'just plain shitting herself'. She had
fallen in love with the natural beauty of the place,
asked what the snap hooks, figure eights and magnesium were for, wanted to know how long the
ropes were and how they attached the bolts to the
rock. She had even climbed some fourteen or fifteen feet before starting to scream in panic. That
night she'd smoked a lot of marijuana, drunk a lot
of wine and joined in teasing him about the fact
that he didn't drink or smoke. She and Keyla,
Renan's girlfriend and pupil, had hit it off and spent

a good hour deep in hushed conversation. Seeing how quickly their partners had become friendly, Renan had started to mumble in his ear. Most of it was unintelligible, but he made out the word 'swing', which was typical of Renan. That night Adri was petulant, incoherent and merry, she had her drunk face on, and he was happy to see her like that. But that was the first and last time she had gone climbing with him. She simply lost interest, as if she'd exhausted every possibility for enjoyment in a single trip. He and Renan had kept going, however. More and more, he needed the endorphins, the adrenaline and the almost meditative mental state of rock climbing. Renan needed to keep on doing what he did best: rising to new challenges on rock faces with the grace of a dancing spider, braving new routes that would be repeated and respected by countless other climbers. And that April day, while resting and admiring the view from the top of Cruz Rock, Renan had asked, without taking his eyes off the landscape, 'Wanna try something totally *Heart of Darkness*?' Still on a high from the climb, he'd been watching a hawk perched on the enormous white cross that gave the place its name. The hawk had just taken flight, flapping its wings against an orange sky streaked with white cloud. 'Try what?' he asked, wrenched out of his daydream. Instead of paying attention to Renan, he began to visualize the descent, which would have to be soon, before it got too dark. Rappelling down was always the part that made him the most nervous. Just as most car accidents take place less than five minutes from the driver's destination, the descent is the part in which a climber is most relaxed, hurried and distracted. Renan waited a few seconds before speaking again. 'Ever thought about ice climbing?' He knew Renan had taken a course in Bariloche and had climbed a few snowy mountains in the Argentinean Andes, which is why he thought he had something in that region in mind. 'I've never thought about it, but it sounds interesting.' 'There's this idea I can't shake, man, a project I can't get out of my head.' 'You want to climb the Aconcagua with your hands tied behind your back?' He expected Renan to laugh, but instead his friend interlaced his fingers and used his right hand to crack the metacarpophalangeal joints of his left, which popped like the little air capsules in bubble wrap. 'I need a partner for a trip, an expedition, actually. Someone who's got the time and is game to invest in some gear, drive for several days, trek out into the middle of nowhere and spend some time on a mountain. Reckon you're up to something like that?' His question seemed to anticipate a negative response and was a subtle challenge, which was common between the two friends when it came to climbing, since Renan was better at the sport in every way and his main motivation was bettering records and feats, preferably other people's. 'Where?' 'The Andes.' 'OK, but have you got a specific mountain in mind?' Renan stopped staring at the horizon and turned to face him. 'Ever heard of Cerro Bonete?' A few neurons sparked in his head, because yes, he had heard of the mountain, in an article in the Canadian magazine *Gripped*, if he wasn't mistaken. A volcanic peak whose summit was some twenty-two thousand feet above sea level, near the Aconcagua in north-eastern Argentina. 'Yeah, I've heard of it,' he replied smugly, feeling like a specialist. 'Isn't it a volcano in Argentina?' 'Yes, well, there's *that* Cerro Bonete, which is near the Aconcagua, in the province of La Rioja. It's twenty-two thousand, one hundred and something feet high and climbers used to turn their noses up at it, but it's become more popular recently. But that's not the one I'm talking about.' Renan feigned nonchalance as he spoke, but he was going somewhere, he obviously wanted to talk about something that had been an object of fascination to him for some time. He paused to create an air of suspense, forcing him to ask, 'So there's another Cerro Bonete, then?' 'There are at least three or four, as far as I know. "Bonete" means some kind of hat in Spanish, and there's a shitload of mountains with the name in the Andes. But the Bonete I'm talking about is special. To begin with, it's in Bolivia. In the south, almost on the Argentinean border.' 'OK. So what's so special about it?' 'It's hard to say, 'cause no one's ever climbed it. It appears on a few maps and in satellite pictures, but its exact height isn't known. I found a page on the net that says it's eighteen thousand, two hundred and forty feet.' 'Not one of the tallest.' 'What matters is that it's unknown. Hardly anything about the region has been documented. There are no roads, no towns, fuck all. The motherfucker is on the edge of a volcanic crater with a three- or four-mile diameter. You should see the aerial photos. There are some on the net. It's awesome.' He knew Renan was serious. Climbing the highest peaks on each continent was already banal to him. Not that they were easy, but lots of people had done them before. He liked to say 'There are package tours to the top of Everest' to illustrate his theory that the true challenges in mountain climbing today were on the most difficult rock faces and on the planet's few mountains that still had a peak or face untouched by ice axes and crampons. An unknown, mysterious mountain would certainly motivate him to leave the comfort of his home and invest in an expedition. Something that hadn't been done before and that deserved to be recorded. His eyes shone as he spoke. He blinked several times in quick succession then held his eyes open for a long time. 'Well? Whadya reckon? Haven't you ever wanted to do something as fucked up as this? It's possible, man, perfectly possible. But it'll take time, money and the right mindset. And balls. I'm just not sure you've got those,' he said, half joking, half serious. 'It's something to think about,' he replied. It seemed like such a crazy idea at the time that he didn't take it seriously. But the following Monday he opened his email at home and found half a dozen messages from Renan full of images of Cerro Bonete and links. The information was sparse and the images were poor-quality satellite photographs taken from obscure geological websites and government reports. One email contained a pair of coordinates and a link to download the program Google Earth. Following the instructions in the email, he installed it, typed in the latitude 21°45'0.00"S and the longitude 66°29'0.00"W, and hit 'Enter'. The three-dimensional globe began to spin slowly as the screen zoomed in on South America and Bolivia, picking up speed as it went. After a few seconds of data transfer, the clear image of a snow-capped peak on the edge of an inactive volcano appeared. His first impression was that he was looking at a map in a very old computer game, but

he slowly understood that it was a legitimate satellite image, with colour and detail, of an incredibly
inhospitable stretch of the Earth's surface. Seen
from above, the texture of the cordillera was like
the bark of an old araucaria tree and the Earth's
crust looked like the crust of a cake, almost palp-
able on the computer screen. And that was when
the idea of the hare-brained expedition took root
in him. Whatever Renan's reasons were, he now
had his own: he needed to go there. He needed that
exact part of the planet to become a place where
he'd set foot, he needed his presence there to be
real. The picture on the screen dredged up mental
images of a range of locations that had sparked
similar urges in him, as if they held some kind of
revelation. He remembered a tiny island he'd seen
while on a boat ride off the southern tip of Santa
Catarina Island, in his first year of marriage. It was
a rocky islet whose top half was covered in vegetation, like so many others along that coast, but on
this one there were three or four wooden huts
facing out to sea, completely isolated, hidden from
the continent. He wondered who had built them,
how they'd got there, if someone actually lived in
those primitive dwellings or if they were just fisher-
men's shacks used for storage and occasional
shelter. Whatever they were, he wanted to be in
one, on an island so removed from civilization. For

an instant it had seemed simple and possible. What was so difficult about picking a deserted corner of the Earth, building a small house on it, and going there from time to time? Later, the idea transformed, revealing itself to be impractical, far less possible than it had first seemed, but letting it go had felt like giving up a valuable opportunity, even though he couldn't define exactly what was so unique or revelatory about that specific place. On another occasion, driving down Highway BR-101 from Torres to Osório, he'd caught sight of a magnificent fig tree on a roadside property and had been gripped by the same feeling of urgency. It would have been the easiest thing in the world to pull over, park, and walk the half mile or so to the tree, sit with his back against the trunk and have some kind of epiphany within minutes of arriving, or merely allow the aura of that particular fig tree on that particular property on that particular highway to slowly fade, return to his car and continue on to Porto Alegre. He'd let that opportunity slip along with dozens of others. What the satellite image on the computer screen offered was another chance to pinpoint a moment in time and space, to the exclusion of all others. He had to go there. If he could have, he'd have beamed himself to the Bolivian Cerro Bonete that very instant. He wrote back to Renan, 'Saw the pics. I'm in (seriously).'

BONOBO

Night was falling on Esplanada. It was early in the new year, and the days still held a trace of the hopeful excitement – of which superstitions and resolutions are part and parcel – that marks the beginning of each new calendar. On the far side of the Guaíba, the red sun was poised to touch the hazy line of hills that was dissolving before his eyes into something like an ocean horizon: the Guaíba River becoming sea, tinged crimson by the setting sun. The weather had been dry and the beaten earth of the football pitch filled the air with a brown dust that hung there, apparently static, for minutes on end, refusing to accept the natural order of things and fall back to the ground. The sounds of players calling for the ball and barking warnings about the other team's defence; of the girls watching the match and noisily making fun of the same guys they would later, face down in bed, cast as the leading men in elaborate sexual fantasies; of the envied scooter owners who revved their engines in exhibitionist duels; and of the children engrossed in their little war games and challenges on the playground equipment in the square – all these swirled together chaotically, the official soundtrack of late-summer-holiday afternoons. In the nearby 8th Mechanized Cavalry Squadron a horse was being broken in and it could be heard whinnying furiously. Behind Hermano was Police Hill, some eight hundred feet high, property of the Brazilian Army. Its partial deforestation had left a landscape of boulders, low-growing grasses, and bushes. Although it was off-limits, it was frequently invaded by adolescents from Esplanada and, less often, adults piggybacking small children. Access to the hill was through the Jungle, a strip of forest teeming with lianas, streams, lizards, snakes, opossums, porcupines and the occasional howler monkey. To Hermano's right, the rest of the square sloped upwards in a series of long, low elevations, with a playground, a *bocce* court, a covered barbecue and a few concrete benches. Hermano saw no harmony in all these elements. They didn't seem to belong to the same physical space – the main square of Esplanada, in this case, which was the name of a residential subdivision but which figured in its inhabitants' psyches as something much grander, like the name of a real suburb. If Esplanada wasn't yet a suburb in its own right, it would be one day. Late afternoon on the football pitch was like a dreamscape cobbled together without much concern for the reality from which it derived. An ocean sunset was impossible in this city, in this country even, but conditioning his eyes to erase the hills fading into the horizon and believe that it was actually happening, that the Guaíba River was the California sea, empowered Hermano's imagination and held reality at bay. He enjoyed it. But reality regained the upper hand with a dirty blow, precise and devastating, when the ball slammed into his nuts at high speed.

'Sorry 'bout that. I was aiming for the goal.' It was Walrus who had kicked the ball clear across the eighty-foot field. He apologized with his head down, puffing, one hand resting on his spare tyre and the other flat on his head. Walrus had more than a hundred nicknames. Kid, Kibe, Pudge, Mouth Tentacles (or just Tentacles), Fat Fool, Senator, Electronics Man, Big Toe, Orson Welles, How Cool Is That, Boobs and dozens of others that Isabela had once compiled into a list in her round handwriting. She had interviewed everyone in Esplanada and delivered the results of her survey to Walrus himself so he could memorize them and respond even when people used the lesser-known ones. But 'Walrus' was sovereign. Although he was fat – not too fat, but fat – and far more walrus-like than most people, it was his Christian name,

Wallace, that had given rise to the nickname. Wallace Wissler. No fourteen-year-old boy had a moustache bigger than his.

The match stopped for a few seconds. Hermano crouched on the field, looking like a sprinter at the start line stricken at the last minute by a terrible headache. Holding his throbbing scrotum with his left hand, he didn't make a sound or utter a word, not even in response to 'Y'OK?' and 'Take it easy, breathe.' He didn't move, experiencing the pain with curiosity. It was as if his testicles had become knotted together, and the slightest movement might activate a muscle or nerve and bring on an unbearable, stabbing pain, in addition to the more diffuse ache spreading from his groin to his thighs and stomach.

They were playing five-a-side. One at the goal and four on the pitch. The score was 'six to them, five to us', as they were now reminded by Bricky (about a year earlier – and no one got what was so funny about it – Bricky had started calling everyone 'Bricky', and had only stopped when people began using it on him), the goalie for Hermano's team and one of his closest friends. The other team members, identified as such by the fact that they were wearing T-shirts, were Uruguay (self-explanatory), Pellet (of unknown origin) and Wagner Montes (after being hit by a vegetable cart on Reservation Street, he'd limped around for two weeks with a horrible cut on his foot that had become infected and oozed secretions of every colour but blue, and when people saw him coming in the distance they'd greet him with the theme song of the talent show on which the real Wagner Montes, who walked with a limp, was a judge). There was no avoiding nicknames in Esplanada. Hermano himself was best known as Horse Hands, because of his extremely long arms and enormous hands, as strong as a Nordic dockworker's, at odds with his fifteen years of age. Bricky whacked the ball upfield into the opposition half, hoping to get it to Uruguay, who was always positioned to attack. Hermano had just stood up, partially recovered, as the ball whizzed over his head. The rival team was playing without shirts and was made up of Walrus, Chrome Black (skin so dark it glinted), the Joker (because of his smile), Mononucleosis (or just Mono, self-explanatory) and Bonobo.

Bonobo was playing well today. He intercepted the ball before it got to Uruguay and dribbled it up the side of the pitch. He was wearing blue nylon shorts and a pair of worn-out football boots. Pellet and Wagner Montes charged at him. Such an open threat of physical contact with Bonobo was only possible in football, though not without misgivings. He continued running with the ball as if there were an empty corridor in front of him, ignoring the fact that a violent collision with the two defenders was imminent. Although he was only five foot seven and thin, except for a reserve of abdominal fat that contrasted grotesquely with the rest of his body, Bonobo moved like a creature twice his weight and size. Other human beings were insignificant obstacles. Everything in existence was an insignificant obstacle. He was always bumping into people and knocking over furniture and potted plants, and never apologized or even turned his head to see if he'd damaged something. He didn't give a shit. He was the kind of guy who'd step on a shard of glass and keep walking around in flip-flops for the rest of the day, totally unfazed, leaving a trail of bloody prints behind him.

The four girls watching the match from the sidelines, sitting atop a mound they referred to as 'the royal box', swung their slender shins and shouted a rehearsed 'Baaahhh' when Bonobo dodged Pellet with a feint to the right and got Wagner Montes out of the way with a shove to the neck that left him gagging, face down on the ground. There was only one opponent left between Bonobo and the goal.

Hermano wasn't so keen on football. He was a mediocre defender who, once or twice a year at most, out of sheer luck, managed to score a goal with a long ball from the far end of the pitch. His reasons for playing were unclear even to him. He liked the physical effort. Being watched sometimes by girls was another undeniable motivation. What attracted him, however, wasn't the game, the competition, or even the interaction with his neighbourhood friends, but the ambience, the setting, the opportunity to be immersed in the atmosphere that enveloped the pitch in the late afternoon. And there was something else. Something that was now hurtling towards him as if deliberately seeking a collision. Something that was staring him in the eye with an intimidating smile. Something to which Hermano only exposed himself so openly on the field, where the very nature of the game brought players' different levels of aggressiveness into alignment. In these matches, Hermano could, to an extent, be physically near Bonobo. He could look at him from close range, study his semi-erect gait and simian features. He could steal the ball from him with a sliding tackle. He could get in his way. As a defender, it was expected that he stop any forward, Bonobo or otherwise, from getting near the goal with the ball at his feet. So Hermano didn't move out of the way or make as if he were about to try some clever footwork as Bonobo barrelled towards him. Instead, he raised his leg and launched himself at Bonobo.

The sound of the resulting collision, which involved very little in the way of sporting technique, echoed throughout the square. An organic, primitive vibration, the contraction of an enormous heart in the centre of the Earth, which stunned the other players, the girls in the royal box, and even some of the children in the playground, who stopped playing and looked at one another as if trying to find the reason for that sudden silence in each other's faces. Bonobo did a full 360 degrees in the air and seemed to float, suspended in the cloud of brown dust for one or two seconds, before hitting the ground and sliding over the rough dirt on his chest, knees and the palms of his hands. He still hadn't come to a complete halt when he leaped up and turned to face Hermano, making it clear that the mistake committed in a few tenths of a second would result in several days of deep regret.

Hermano's first reaction was to avoid eye contact with Bonobo. He instinctively glanced at Bricky, who had frozen mid-wince in the middle of the goal, his face contorted in a mixture of terror and resignation.

'That's right, don't look at me,' snarled Bonobo. 'If you look me in the eye, you'll be shitting your own teeth in the morning.' The threat was rhetorical, but coming from Bonobo each word was a deep thud driving a hypothetical nail into a hypothetical wall. To disobey would be too risky, but Hermano wanted to. He wanted to look, but he hesitated. Bricky, whose eyes were still locked with his and who knew what he was thinking, opened his eyes even wider and shook his head slightly, trying to stress that defiance was a very, very bad idea. Hermano glanced down at the ground, at Police Hill, at a glider crossing the pink sky, respecting the silence of the square. He glanced at a whole bunch of things, except Bonobo, who was standing about six feet away. Meanwhile, Uruguay, Chrome Black and Wagner Montes positioned themselves between the two to reduce the chance of visual and/or physical contact, while Mononucleosis, the owner of the ball, tucked it under his arm and sidled away to force the match to end, disperse the players and make a fight less likely. The girls came down from the royal box to get a closer view of what was going on. Isabela, Lara and Ingrid kept away from the centre of the conflict, standing on the sideline as if it were a safety barrier, Isabela holding Lara's arm, and Lara's fingertips resting on Ingrid's plump waist, all as curious as they were tense. Only the most petite and slender of the four, Naiara, dared set foot on the pitch. She approached Bonobo.

'Hey.'

Hermano was now testing the limits of his

peripheral vision, his eyes trained on a spot on the ground halfway between him and Bonobo. It was the borderline of disobedience. Moving his eyes just a little further towards Bonobo would be taken as a response to his challenge.

'Hey!'

The presence of Naiara and her shrill thirteen-year-old girl's voice trying to get her brother's attention only made Hermano want to look at Bonobo even more – and to hell with the consequences. He tried to control his breathing and weigh up the pros and cons of a range of possible responses, but the simple fact that he was thinking too much meant he wasn't really ready to face his opponent. The realization paralysed him once and for all.

'Hey, bro, let it go. He didn't do it on purpose. He's clumsy.'

'Butt out.'

It was the last thing Bonobo said. Afterwards, Hermano stood there staring at the ground for he didn't know how long, absorbed by the absence of thought in his mind. Ten seconds or ten minutes might have passed before Bricky put his hand on his shoulder and said that everyone had gone. Mononucleosis had taken off with the ball and the match was over, Bonobo had disappeared up the square with Chrome Black and Uruguay, and the girls had gone too. Only the children were still there, spinning around on the merry-go-round.

For his thirteenth birthday, Hermano's parents had given him a metal tin of Swiss Caran d'Ache watercolour pencils. The tin was red and cold to the touch, approximately fifteen by ten inches, and contained two plastic trays, each of which held forty pencils. The outside of the pencils faithfully reproduced their actual colours, and the eighty different shades lined up in the trays formed smooth, luminous progressions of colour. It was hypnotizing, so beautiful that Hermano had been reluctant to even touch them for a few days, as if disturbing their order might break a spell. The present was imported and had cost a small fortune. On the back of the tin was the product description in twenty-three languages. Although Hermano himself couldn't remember it, his parents assured him that at some point in his early childhood he had emphatically declared that he wanted to be a painter when he grew up. A few days after his birthday, when he had plucked up the courage to take a few pencils out of the tin, he'd tried to draw a few things on Canson paper. He'd tested each colour and used a small paintbrush dipped in water to experiment with water-colouring. After a few weeks of scribbling and attempting to explore the pencil collection as an artistic instrument, he had stuffed the tin into the bottom of a desk drawer and never brought it out again. The sheets of Canson paper that had figured in Hermano's short-lived career as a painter still existed, stored away in a folder. There were a few attempts at drawing, a pig's face here, a tree there, a Saturn-like planet, and poorly copied scenes of violence from comic books, but for the most part the pages were filled with doodles that made no sense, little blotches of saturated colour, experiments with layering, places where the paper had torn because there had been too much water on the brush, gradations of colour, cross-hatching.

When he walked into his room after the incident on the field, Hermano remembered the tin of pencils, sentenced to oblivion at the bottom of the drawer more than two years earlier. He fished it out from under a pile of old textbooks and other classroom material, sat at his desk, opened it and stared at the pencils. Although most of the tips were a little spent, none had ever been sharpened. They lay there neatly in their original sequence. The top tray comprised predominantly reds, pinks, blues, greys, black. The bottom one, yellows, greens, browns, beiges and special tones of gold and silver. He left the tin open on the white Formica desktop.

He peeled off his T-shirt, trainers and socks and

sat on the bed. His clothes were soaked with sweat, and Porto Alegre's muggy summer heat kept him perspiring heavily, even though his body was now relaxed. In addition to the desk, there was also a single bed with an iron frame in the room, a wall-to-wall wardrobe and a little table with a 14" colour TV and a Nintendo video-game console sitting on it. Shelves on the wall over his bed held a modest collection of children's books, teen fiction and classics, a helicopter and half a dozen G.I. Joe action figures (Flash, Rock 'n Roll, Zap, Glider Pilot, Short-Fuze and Cobra Officer), four He-Men (Prince Adam, Orko, Ram Man and Mer-Man) and other children's toys abandoned not so long ago. On another wall, a *Mad Max 2: The Road Warrior* poster showed Mel Gibson in black leather holding a sawn-off shotgun. Bricky had got it for him, as his parents owned a video rental shop. The sound system had been broken for about a year. Comic books, porn and video-game magazines were stacked in a corner. The room looked as if it had been unoccupied for a long time. Although it was never particularly tidy, it wasn't a picture of seismic devastation like most teenagers' bedrooms.

Hermano pulled a pair of six-pound iron dumb-bells out from under the bed. With a weight in each hand, he stood in front of the mirror behind the door and began pumping his arms in alternating bicep curls. He did two sets of twenty reps for each arm. Then he dropped down to the worn beige carpet and did thirty push-ups. When he stood up again, the waistband of his shorts was drenched with sweat. He looked at himself in the mirror for a few seconds. The veins in his forearms were visible, palpitating. With his feet planted on the ground, he turned to each side, examining the muscles in his back, around his ribs, his calves. He spent some time adjusting his position until the mirror reflected back a casual stance, not the pose of one who is studying his own image. His arms and knees were covered in cuts and scrapes, some still raw and recent, others dark scabs that were already coming loose. Elsewhere, recently healed wounds had left patches of pink, sensitive skin. His body was slim and well proportioned. Only his arms looked longer than they ought to. His muscles were firm but not bulging. His brown skin was covered with short hair only partially darkened by age.

Suddenly, the image of Bonobo sliding across the ground on his chest lit up in his memory, eliciting a snort of laughter, because seen from a distance like that it was pretty funny, just as Bricky's gaping face framed by the goalposts was also funny. As he recalled what happened next, however, he ceased to find it funny and was filled with loathing and frustration. He didn't really know why he had gone for Bonobo like that. His actions had been instinctive and gratuitous. The worst part wasn't that he'd kept his eyes glued to the ground. It was that he'd taken the initiative *himself*, sticking his heel out and throwing the entire weight of his body against his opponent. Avoiding Bonobo's glare was the reaction you'd expect from most people – except perhaps Uruguay, who wasn't afraid of anyone and considered physical strength one of the main attributes of the people of his straight-highwayed little country – but provoking Bonobo *and then* chickening out of the fight was inexcusable and humiliating. He had acted like a stray dog that, traumatized from a beating or an accident, barks furiously at anything that moves then sticks its tail between its legs and curls up like an armadillo, cowering under a car at the slightest sign of aggression. Bonobo had no shoulders. His head looked like an oversized bean perched atop a triangular torso held in place by a tyre of fat. He had short little tyrannosaurus arms. Everyone thought he looked like Horácio from the *Turma da Mônica* comic books, but no one dared tell anyone else for fear it might get back to Bonobo, so they all thought they were the only ones to make the secret comparison and chuckled to themselves whenever they thought about it. But despite his almost deformed appearance and thuggish behaviour, it was impossible not to fall under Bonobo's spell. No matter how much fear or repulsion he inspired in others, any interaction with him felt like a privilege. From any point of view, no matter what the circumstances, messing with him in a football match was just plain stupid.

Hermano's BO was so nauseating that he was actually beginning to feel queasy. Even during summer break, there comes a day when a man must wash. He took the tin of pencils from the desk, walked a few paces down the corridor and locked himself in the bathroom.

He turned on the tap and splashed cold water on his face. Instead of getting straight into the shower, he sat on the toilet lid and began to speculate about what the consequences might have been if he'd returned Bonobo's stare. Hermano had never been in a real fight. He'd been hurt in countless ways, all over his body, and in some cases his parents had had to take him to the hospital for stitches or an X-ray. He had smashed face-first into trees, fallen off the swing and landed on his chin, taken horrific spills from bicycles, buried a fishing hook in his inner thigh, split fingernails in half, torn several soft parts of his flesh on rusty barbed wire and broken a tooth on a bus turnstile. But he couldn't imagine what it felt like to be punched in the face.

He made a fist and pressed it into his cheek, his mouth, the tip of his nose, first gently, then pressing the bones of his hand hard into his flesh, imagining the kind of pain that might be involved in a hypothetical run-in with Bonobo. The feeling of punching someone else in the face was equally mysterious.

The tin of pencils was sitting on the counter and for a moment Hermano wasn't sure how it had come to be there, until he remembered he had brought it there himself for no particular reason.

He lifted the lid and ran his fingers over the reds, which rolled on their axes, comfortably accommodated in their plastic grooves. He turned on the tap just enough to let a silent, unmoving thread of water run from its mouth and disappear into the plughole. There were five shades of red in the tin. He chose the darkest, next to the burgundy, and held the tip of the water-soluble pencil under the stream for a few seconds. Still sitting on the toilet lid, he drew a straight line across the back of his left hand. It left a bright-red mark. He stared at it for a few seconds, then stood and positioned himself in front of the mirror. His heartbeat quickened a little. The agitation he felt reminded him of the first time he'd shut himself away to masturbate, his imagination awash with unfathomable outcomes. He wet his whole face with his hands, rubbing away the crust of salt left by the dried sweat on his forehead and around his mouth. He took the same pencil and painted a small area of his upper lip red. He wasn't satisfied with the result. It looked like the crappy make-up in late-night TV movies. He decided that just one red wasn't going to do the job. The tin offered a whole range of tones, and realism could only be achieved by combining them. He tried applying each of the different reds on top of one another. He tested a few pinks, burgundy, and soon he had a convincing ruby-red. But something was still missing. There couldn't be blood without a wound. With a sharp navy-blue he drew a small dark line, which soon bled partially into the surrounding red. He put a bit more red over it and took a step back. If someone had come into the bathroom at that moment, they'd have thought he had a real cut on his upper lip. The still-wet paint beaded and ran down to his lower lip, where it spread to his incisors. The effect, which was very realistic, brought to mind a frenetic sequence of images from films and comics, a montage of wounded heroes – Elektra being beaten by sadistic cyborgs, the young Veto Skreemer's face slashed by a razor, Robert De Niro with a bullet wound in the neck, a bloody Mad Max dragging himself out of his black Ford Falcon after a spectacular roll, samurai, gangsters and avengers from TV screens and the pages of graphic novels, who didn't just bleed, but wore their blood like warpaint, giving their stoicism a holy dimension. Now he was the blood-soaked hero, staring out of the toothpaste-splattered mirror. Bonobo had just punched him in the face, knocking him to the ground on the football pitch, but he got up and stared his adversary in the eye. He crouched on the bathroom floor and stood slowly, hands on the edge of the sink. His face appeared in the mirror in slow motion, greasy, wet and wounded, bloody saliva covering his teeth. Bonobo took another swing at him, but he dodged and got him in an arm lock, skilfully using the intuitive martial art he had developed over years of street fighting. He planted a well-aimed blow in Bonobo's face. Bricky came to his aid, but he told him to stand back. The girls were screaming for them to stop. But now he was grappling with Bonobo again, throwing and taking punches in turn. The red pencils worked with precision on his wet face, making a cut in his brow, giving colour and flow to a nosebleed. When he layered on enough paint in one spot and then added a drop or two of water, a trickle of blood would streak down his skin. Every time he was hit in the face, he simulated the impact, throwing his head to one side, and the blood splattered on to the bathroom door and the glass of the shower cubicle. Drops of red plopped into the sink, reminiscent of the real blood that had marked the white porcelain on other occasions, cuts on his fingers, hands and feet that needed to be washed and disinfected. He took such a beating that the blood was now streaming down his chest and had splattered over most surfaces in the bathroom. He imagined the bones of his face breaking under Bonobo's grazed fists, onlookers gathered in a semicircle around the fight, silently watching the loser's complete destruction.

'Hermano?'

He stopped. The door was splattered with red. His neck and chest were covered with red paint. The sink was completely red. The floor was red.

'Everything OK in there?'

'I'm fine, Mum.'

'I heard noises.'

'It's nothing. I'm going to have a shower.'

He used an entire roll of toilet paper, water and soap to clean the bathroom. Then he turned off the water heater and took a cold shower. Paint mixed with water tinged the floor tiles red for the first minute. Then the water ran clean. He felt ashamed, not really because of the scene he had just staged and starred in, but because he had lost a fight scripted in his own imagination.

6.13 A.M.

On the Tuesday morning he read Renan's reply: 'good to hear, faggot! the mountain's ours!!!! come to the gym today so we can talk. u seen the new babe in spin class?!!?? if u haven't, u'll see her today. c. u. renam.' Renan was the kind of guy who spelled his own name wrong. But few people in Brazil could climb as well as he could, and that night he discovered that his friend had more than enough know-how and logistical wherewithal to plan an expedition like the one they intended to undertake. Driving up Nilo Peçanha towards Carlos Gomes Avenue, he slowed from fifty-five to thirty miles an hour twenty yards from the electronic speed bump and heard his enormous backpack roll across the boot, a compact mass of camping accessories, mountain- and ice-climbing gear, special clothes, food, electronic equipment – a bundle of items that had been methodically researched, bought and packed, and included a tent for two and a sleeping bag for temperatures as low as minus twenty, thermal insulation, a benzine camping stove, benzine,

plastic soft-drink bottles (the lightest, most prac-
tical, cheapest canteens of all), cutlery, two small
titanium pans, a torch, batteries, a pocket knife,
water-purifying tablets, a lighter, matches, plastic
bags of different sizes, sealable bags for clothes and
fragile equipment, painkillers, muscle relaxants, a
first-aid kit, dried fruit, chocolate, muesli bars, rice,
lentils, sticks of beef jerky, a range of tinned foods,
a toiletry bag containing the most basic of personal-
hygiene items, four pairs of underwear, three
T-shirts, a pair of trousers, a pair of shorts, three
layers of special clothing for climbing in low temperatures, starting with thermal underwear made
of polyester up against the body to absorb sweat,
then a layer of fleece, and over the top a moisture-
wicking anorak that allowed perspiration to
evaporate while remaining waterproof, as well as a
hood, gloves, special protective glasses, a neck
warmer, sunblock, lip balm, a 7.2 megapixel digital
camera, an iPod, a GPS, a notebook, not to mention
the actual climbing gear, such as static and
dynamic dry ropes of different lengths, a helmet, a
rappel seat, snap hooks, slings, figure eights, rock-
climbing shoes, double boots for ice, an ice axe,
crampons, and a host of other things that might be
needed at base camp and during the climb, while
also striving to keep weight to a minimum. Renan
had all kinds of tricks to reduce the overall weight

of the backpacks, from cutting the tags out of every item of clothing and breaking off toothbrush handles to opting for 9.8-millimetre ropes, the thinnest considered safe for that kind of climb: apparently insignificant measures but which all together could take a few pounds off their backs. For five months they had stockpiled the gear they would need and mapped out the route, drawing a jittery line of state and federal highways that would take them through the Gaucho Highlands, across the states of Santa Catarina, Paraná and Mato Grosso do Sul, where they planned to cross the Bolivian border and then drive up the treacherous, winding roads to Potosí at almost thirteen thousand feet on the Bolivian Plateau, where they would stop for a few days before travelling the remaining two hundred and twenty miles to the Cerro Bonete region. According to their calculations, they would still need to hike another four or five miles through valley floors to the foot of the mountain, where they would set up their base camp. At first, Adri had had a few unforgettable fits of hysteria. She had disapproved of the expedition from the outset, and it took her a few weeks to realize it wasn't just a passing obsession. First she'd tried to convince him that it was a ridiculous waste of money, and the amount he'd have to invest in it all really did place the project in the category of eccentricities. Renan had obtained partial sponsorship from a brand of backpacks and sporting gear. The contract stipulated that the company logo or name should appear explicitly in all publicity, as well as in photographs of the expedition and a range of other situations that were described in minute detail. It lightened the financial burden, but Adri had quickly realized that the financial argument wasn't going to change his mind anyway, since money hadn't been a concern for them for at least two years. They were doing fine. So she had changed tack and begun a campaign of psychological pressure and emotional blackmail, pointing out the danger and unpredictability of the journey and stressing that neither of them, not even Renan, who was a professional, had enough experience to take on something so extreme. But he had replied over and over that the daring and risk were part of what had appealed to him in the first place. Her last resort revealed the true nature of her feelings. 'You've got a daughter, I hope you haven't forgotten that too,' she said abruptly one night, shortly after arriving home from a new Italian restaurant in Moinhos de Vento and relieving the babysitter. They were sitting in the kitchen, just before bed, as he drank a glass of water with a few drops of lime juice and she smoked one of the latest low-yield cigarettes. He'd been waiting for the selfish-irresponsible-father-with-a-child-to-raise approach and was ready to strike back with a mixture of indignation, reassurance, existential insights and attempts to pump up his opponent's self-esteem, but what caught his attention was the 'too' at the end of the sentence. The word came out crooked, her voice trailing off. It wasn't part of what she had planned to say. And there could only be one thing that he was forgetting *too*. He wanted to jump out of the chair and hug her tight, but he'd learned that hugs only resolved things temporarily and weren't remembered later. Hugs were impotent. She wanted him to give up what he was doing for her. It was a plea. But what about his own dreams? He had hoped, until a few minutes ago, that she'd admit that deep down she knew how important it was to him, give him a long goodbye kiss and say that she understood and would be there waiting for him to come back, and that she'd tell Nara that her dad had gone to do something very brave but that he'd be fine and would be back in a few weeks with presents from the Indians in Bolivia and photos of a volcano crater that no one else had ever photographed at close range. But neither of them had given in. He hadn't decided not to go, and she had pretended to be asleep when he left. Now it was too late. He turned right on to Carlos Gomes, recently widened and resurfaced with an almost white concrete that made him remember, absurdly, the strip of white sand lit by the headlights of his dad's Fiat Tempra some six years earlier, when he'd left a party with Adri in the middle of the night and, instead of taking her home, had driven over twenty miles to Lami Beach because she'd said she wanted to be alone with him, far away from everything and everyone. They'd known each other for about two months and for the first time in his life, at the age of twenty-four, in the home stretch of his medical degree at the Federal University, he had begun to question his certainty that he would remain single, a perspective that contained a small amount of resignation and just as much intention. He didn't see how living with a woman could make his life any better, and his brief experiences with girlfriends had only drained him of enormous amounts of energy that he believed vital to his primary objectives, which at the time were his studies, his quest to become an outstanding surgeon, and maintaining his impeccable physical form and stamina. Just imagining a long, hypocritical courting ritual caused him more anxiety than any university exam, and it didn't help that he was the only sober person at the rare parties he forced himself to attend. It wasn't the first time he'd been intimate with a woman, but it was the first time he'd been *with* one. She was the same age as him, was studying Fine Arts after dropping out of Pharmaceutical Science, and used to joke that she needed a man who was going to become a wealthy doctor to bankroll her creative whims until she became internationally famous. She was pretty, inconvenient and enchanting. He took her to Lami, parked on the sand in a secret spot he knew, about fifty yards from the water, and they spent the rest of the night probing the boundaries of each other's personal histories and bodies, pulling back the moment before revisiting difficult experiences or doing anything that could actually be classified as fucking, as if it might destroy the almost euphoric state of happiness that hummed inside the car and seemed to depend on a delicate balance of factors. The radio was tuned to Continental and, suddenly, right after something that may well have been Ray Conniff, a lesser-known song by Pink Floyd came on. He had heard 'Fearless' on vinyl at some point in his adolescence and it had become his soundtrack for moments of solitary meditation. Adri climbed on to his lap in the driver's seat and started shaking out her black hair, which at the time came down almost to her waist. She predicted that they'd be together for a long time and explained why she was absolutely fascinated by the art philosophy course she was taking that semester. At some stage he realized he was screwed and that keeping her happy had just been added to his small list of primary objectives. And he felt the need to say it. 'You know how

you're feeling right now?' 'What about it?' 'I want
to make you keep on feeling like this for as long as
possible.' Approximately one year later, weeks after
his graduation, they were married, living in an old
one-bedroom apartment that belonged to his
mother, on a nice street in the suburb of Petrópolis.
And now, if the truth be known, his intent to extend
the happiness of the hours they spent at Lami Beach
for as long as possible could be considered his biggest failure, because nothing remotely like that had
ever happened again. Their life together had passed
quickly and on automatic pilot. They'd spent little
time together in the first few years; he, busy with
medical residencies and post-grad courses, one in
São Paulo, as well as excruciatingly rigorous scien-
tific reading and long runs at night, which were the
only way to buoy his spirits, stay disciplined and
keep his sights set on his objectives; she, increasingly involved with artists and 'creative people', as
she called them with open mockery, helping her
painter friends put on exhibitions, and slowly creating her own works that sought to 'explore vegetable
matter to expose the biological nervure that the
urban landscape conceals beneath tarmac and concrete', as he clearly remembered reading in a flyer
for a joint exhibition held in an old renovated mansion where she'd exhibited a composition of
fragments of paving that had been broken up by

tree roots, as well as root segments that had been removed by the Department for the Environment for the same reason and, finally, the crowd-pleaser: part of a *Tipuana* tree trunk, in which slabs of pavement, a chrome car bumper and an improbable plate of glass were embedded like shrapnel from a grenade, painstakingly assembled with the use of chisels, drills and a small electric saw. The trunk still oozed sap and resin, and there was a strange beauty to the arrangement, beyond the obvious environmentalist reading. The piece earned her an invitation to the Porto Alegre Biennial at the end of the year. She had deferred her university enrolment one semester before graduating, alleging that she didn't need the diploma but she did need time to work on her next creation, about which she refused to reveal a thing, except to a few of her artist friends. The pre-Biennial press coverage noted the mystery surrounding the work of artist Adriane Weissmann, a promising new local talent. A large shed was built beside the Guaíba River, near Harmonia Park, to house the installation. 'Does it have to do with trees?' he had asked her on one occasion, and it was the only thing she revealed before the exhibition opened. 'Yes.' What his wife had done was dig up an amazing specimen of *Ficus benjamina*, a species of fig tree that sent out roots over an enormous area, destroying walls and paving. She'd sawn

off the treetop and had hung the intact trunk and
roots from the ceiling of the shed, making people
look up. It was mind-boggling. You couldn't exactly
say that the tree – which she had been allowed to
uproot from a property in Viamão only after a series
of municipal authorizations and environmental
compensation agreements – had been torn up.
Rather, it had been surgically removed from the
ground in a patient and meticulous excavation that
had preserved its enormous, winding roots almost
to perfection, a job she'd finished just two days
before the Biennial opened. She'd had to cut the tree
into several parts in order to transport it, and then
reassemble it with the help of diagrams and photographs. The public entered the shed through a
narrow door and found the floor strewn with shiny
fig leaves. There was a panel showing the many
different meanings and symbolisms associated with
fig trees. In the Bible, after eating the forbidden
fruit, Adam and Eve cover themselves with fig
leaves. In ancient Greece, the tree was associated
with Athena, and the exportation of its fruit was
forbidden. In ancient Rome, it was considered a
sacred symbol of Romulus, and the fig had an erotic
connotation, associated with Priapus. In India, the
Ficus religiosa is the holiest of trees, and according
to Vedic legend it is inhabited by Brahma, Vishnu
and Maheshwara, thus symbolizing the Hindu

triad. In a number of cultures it is a symbol of abundance or immortality. And so on – not forgetting, either, that the majestic fig tree in the Pampas is an icon of the gaucho landscape of Brazil's deep south. Overhead, lit by narrow windows set in all four walls of the shed, the public could see the intricate and vaguely radial structure of the gigantic roots reaching through space, as if the tree had been planted in the air. It was breathtaking, and long queues formed at the entrance. There were protests, articles offering the most disparate interpretations, and newspaper surveys asking if it was a brilliant work of art, sheer stupidity or an environmental crime. Despite the repercussions, Adri refused to give interviews and, to his complete dismay, declared that she was done with the art world for ever. She had simply lost interest. It was always the same with his wife and the mother of his child: she lost interest. Shortly before she became pregnant, she and two friends had opened a clothing shop, but Adri had opted out of the partnership a few months later. The shop closed a year later. Then she had worked as art director on a short film by a local director. Before they had even finished shooting, she would come home in a state of stress, promising that she never wanted to see those people again and cursing film-making everywhere and for all time. Then she fell pregnant and it was as if motherhood had prematurely torn her from a long process of experimentation and indecision that seemed far from over. He often wondered when she was simply going to tire of him, and sometimes suspected that it had already happened, a long time earlier, shortly after they were married or perhaps before. But he knew that there was still something holding them together besides their daughter. He might have lost hope of restoring in her the sheer happiness that had steamed up the car windows that night on Lami Beach, but he couldn't bear to see her in pain, not even a little, for whatever reason, and he felt capable of doing anything to end her suffering. Recently, lying on the bed while he did sit-ups on the floor, she had looked up from the novel she was reading and said, 'My life is like musical chairs, except back-to-front. Whenever the music stops they add more chairs.' He could try to add chairs, if there weren't enough. But how did you remove chairs from someone's life? How could he choose for her? He still loved her, he was entirely certain of it. But it was a rational love. He knew exactly why he loved her, and had countless reasons for them to stay together. She no doubt felt similarly. For a host of reasons that they kept to themselves, they continued to choose, day after day, to stay where they were.

THE HILL

'Looks like the sky's going to cave in any minute now.'

Bricky stopped with his foot on a rock and looked up, frowning. They had hiked the first two hundred yards of the trail up Police Hill, after crossing the Jungle. A compact mass of clouds covered the sky. The hot, hazy light they gave off seemed to be slowly cooking the plants. Even out in the open, the feeling was oppressive. Hermano looked at the clouds and calculated that it would be at least two hours before the rain came. Still staring at the sky, he said in a deep voice, imitating TV dubbing:

'*But what IS important is gravity!*'

Bricky chuckled and responded with the same diction:

'*Sully, remember when I promised I would kill you last?*'

Hermano added in a high-pitched voice:

'*That's right, Matrix, you did!*'

'*I lied.*'

'*Aaaaaahhhh . . .*'

Laughter.

'Anyone want a beer?' asked Uruguay, who was carrying a cooler full of ice and cans of beer on his shoulder.

'No.'

'No.'

'No, thanks.'

'Can I have a sip?' said Isabela.

'Anything for you, babe.'

'You don't give up, do you?'

Hermano didn't answer Uruguay. They all knew he didn't drink. He was walking with Naiara and Bricky. A little further back were Uruguay and Isabela, who was now taking a rebellious swig from the can of beer. Pellet brought up the rear, zigzagging as he walked, convinced he deserved someone's attention.

'Did I tell you guys I had datura tea in Riozinho?'

'Shut your face and hold the cooler for me, Pellet.'

'Do we have to go under the barbed wire?'

'Yep, I'll hold it up for you.'

'You know there's a datura tree at the Joker's place, don't you? The flower looks like a bell, like this. White. There's a whole tree full of the shit in his garden. It's the biggest trip ever, dude. A total head spin.'

'The wire's rusty.'

'Can someone help me here?'

'Go on, Horse Hands, give Naiara a *hand*.'

Hermano helped Naiara under the barbed wire that Bricky was holding up for them. Her hand was so small and slender that he was afraid to hold it too tight.

'Thanks.'

'We almost there?'

'Want me to carry you, Isabela?'

'Hands off me, Uruguay. Off.'

'I'm just trying to help.'

'Does this hill really belong to the army?' asked Naiara. Her wavy black hair was pulled back in a ponytail. She was wearing a white top with spaghetti straps and denim shorts. On her feet, brown flip-flops with a padded thong. They were all in flip-flops, except Uruguay, who had on a pair of leather sandals.

'It does,' replied Bricky, 'but they don't use this part for anything. The barracks are on the other side. They ride horses and train over there.'

'How are you guys going to get out of military service?' asked Isabela breathlessly.

'I'm not. I'm going to enlist.'

'Bricky always has to be the black sheep.'

'But I want to. The pay's good.'

'*Good* is learning how to use a gun,' said

Uruguay, stopping to put his empty beer can in the cooler and take out a new one.

'My brother wants to enlist too,' said Naiara. 'We've got a second cousin who was in the army and he told us all kinds of stuff, and my brother thought it sounded cool. They dumped him in the middle of the forest with some other soldiers and left them there for a week with nothing to eat. They had to eat roots, grubs. Drink rainwater. After a week they threw them in a hole full of chickens and they were so hungry they killed the chickens with their bare hands and ate them raw. It totally grossed me out.'

Uruguay opened the new can, letting a gurgling jet of carbon dioxide and foam escape.

'What about you, Hands?' said Naiara, hopping from stone to stone, trying not to step on the ground.

'What?'

'Are you going to join the army?'

Hermano had never thought about it. In fact, he didn't really understand what the others were talking about. He found the whole concept of the army weird.

'Dunno. It's still a while off.'

'You should serve, Hands. "Strong arm, friendly *hand*."'

'With those *hands* in the armed forces, the country's sovereignty is guaranteed.'

'Horse Hands is going to university, that's for sure.'

'The hell he is. Hands is going to be an actor. The sort that doesn't say a word.'

'Ha, tell me 'bout it!'

'Those movies where the lead actor doesn't say a thing.'

'I've never seen one like that.'

'*Death Wish* is like that.'

'So is *Cobra*. If Hands pumped some iron, he could go to Hollywood.'

'"*You're a disease and I'm the cure.*"'

'Or he could be a stuntman.'

'That too. If he doesn't kill himself on his bike first.'

'I reckon we're pissing him off.'

'You pissed off, Hands?'

'Yeah, he doesn't like being the centre of attention.'

'Hands is pissed off. He's crappy.'

Laughter.

'Ever seen a baby's face when it's taken a crap?'

'He's going to keep his mouth shut and pretend not to hear us until we stop.'

'But we're never going to stop, just to see what happens.'

'Nothing's going to happen. He's going to stay quiet and crappy.'

'He's walking faster to get away from us.'

'I ran home with the bag of datura flowers and thought I'd invite Chrome Black to come have the tea with me. But the last time he didn't drink much, so it hardly had any effect, and he was a pain in the arse, saying I was talking to people that weren't there and doing stupid things. He just sat there on his skateboard, rocking back and forth and laughing at me, and I didn't know why. So I thought "Fuck Chrome" and decided to go to Riozinho by myself. Solo. Hey, have you guys ever noticed that even Chrome's teeth are kinda black?'

'Fuck, Pellet's going on about datura tea again,' groaned Bricky.

'Just ignore him.'

'My mum calls that flower "angel's trumpet",' said Isabela. 'When I was little she told me it was so poisonous that if I got anywhere near one I'd drop dead on the spot. You didn't even have to touch it, just being close was enough. I used to dream about the tree and wet the bed.'

'Have you guys seen that movie where the tree rapes a woman?'

'*The Evil Dead*. The one with the book made of human flesh.'

'So I got my backpack ready, took the bag of flowers, a bottle of cachaça, and a brick of weed I'd bought from Agenor, and caught the bus to

Riozinho. I took some alcohol to start a fire and a pot to make the tea in. And a two-litre bottle of mineral water. I just wanted to go away somewhere and get shit-faced, you know? But when I got off in Riozinho early that afternoon, the place was full of campers and day-trippers. There were people swimming in the river and some fugly chicks roasting their arses in the sun, covered in gnat bites. Horror show. I tried several different places along the river, but whenever I found a nice spot there'd be a bunch of dickheads having a barbecue and blundering about in the water. You know the ones who look like they're drowning when they try to swim? So I thought "Fuck this" and headed for Canastra Hill.'

Pellet's story was a monologue that didn't require his listeners to respond – or even exist for that matter. The prevailing theory was that the weekend in Riozinho had nuked most of Pellet's brain, sparing only the part that controlled vital functions and the neurons that stored memories of his experience on Canastra Hill. He was thin and wiry and didn't look built to handle all the substances he claimed to consume. His blond hair was clipped in a bowl cut. Every now and then someone got a fright when they turned around and found him staring at the back of their neck, gesticulating.

The trail was getting steeper now. The clouds seemed closer to their heads. Not a leaf moved and the birds had all disappeared and gone quiet. The most distinct noise was the sound of buses accelerating on avenues miles away.

'There's a trail that goes from the dirt road in Riozinho up to the top of Canastra Hill. It's about a three-hour hike. It's fucking high – any of you ever been? It's like three of this hill here, stacked on top of one another. It's all dense forest. The trail's insane. Hardly anyone goes there. Some parts are almost vertical. You've got to hold on to vines as you go, sort of rock climbing in places. But I didn't give a shit. I needed to chill, you know? And if there's a place in this world to chill, it's up on Canastra Hill. I put my backpack on, got my tent and went. You shoulda seen all the mosquitoes on the trail. Mud everywhere. When the mosquitoes came swarming at me I'd get ten, fifteen bites in a matter of seconds and sometimes I'd slip in the mud. It was sick. I tied a T-shirt round my face and the bastards managed to bite me *through* the T-shirt. Mosquitosauruses. I was such a wreck after every mosquito attack that I'd have to sit on a rock for a few minutes and smoke a joint. I almost put my weed supply in jeopardy 'cause of the little motherfuckers.'

'You avoiding me, Isabela?'

'You're like a rash today, Uruguay.'

'I just want to talk. You don't know how much you need me.'

'Oh, God.'

'Jesus, Uruguay.'

'Hey, Hands, there's a horsefly on your back.'

Hermano stopped and swatted his own back with the T-shirt he was holding. The fly flew away.

'Thanks, Naiara.'

'If one of them gets you, the blood from the bite attracts others.'

'When I got to the top the sun was setting. Awesome view. Not a soul for miles around. I found a part of the hill where the slope looked to be less than forty-five degrees and pitched my tent. I picked a spot with a kind of wall of bushes, with grass and bamboo underneath. If I tripped over, the bushes would stop me rolling all the way to the bottom. A dude's gotta think of everything. I pitched the tent and sat there a while, just having a puff and drinking the cachaça. To put a shine on things.'

'Do we go right or left here?'

'Left. We're almost there.'

'I lit a fire before it got dark. If I moved even a short distance away, everything disappeared. Pitch black. There was no moon. A strong wind started up. Good thing I'd piled up plenty of firewood. After two or three joints, I got the munchies. But I'd thought of everything. You gotta plan. Trips like this aren't worth it if you don't plan ahead. On the way there the bus had stopped at a fruit stand in Morungava and I'd bought a huge hunk of yellow cheese. It must have weighed four or five pounds, the cheese. When the munchies hit me, I attacked the cheese. I ate half of it. You can't be low on energy if you're going to drink datura tea. Planning! If you guys ever drink datura tea, plan it all ahead of time. Take it from me.'

'Somebody make him stop.'

'So I made the tea. I filled a can with alcohol and set it on fire so I could heat the water in the pot. When I went to put in the flowers, I saw that they were kinda wilted and ugly. I'd always used perky, white flowers before. I was afraid the tea would be weak, that it wouldn't work well with the flowers all wilted like that. So I used the whole lot, double the amount I'd used before, and gave them a good squeeze just to be sure. And then I drank that shit. Knocked it all back in one go. It was only after I'd swallowed it that I realized it tasted stronger than usual. It was like dirty water, boiled potato skins, something like that. Kinda gross, to be honest. I squatted by the fire and waited for it to hit me. I had a bit of cachaça and rolled another spliff to pass the time. And nothing happened. I reckon a half hour or an hour went past – I didn't have a watch on. Nothing happened. I'd smoked half my weed and there was only an inch of cachaça at the bottom of the bottle. I could hear the branches of the trees swaying in the wind, a scary sound that only reminded me that that was no place for people. There were just spiders, monkeys and snakes in the forest. And the tea didn't take effect. I began to think that wilted flowers don't work. All I'd done was drink dirty water. I didn't have any cigarettes, a Walkman, or anyone to talk to. Then something dawned on me. The other times I'd had the tea, I'd always had someone with me. Usually Chrome Black. And it was the people around me who'd told me that I was really shit-faced, that I was acting like a retard, that I'd put my bike on my bed so my mum would think I was asleep, that I'd laugh for no reason, that I'd ask for a cigarette every thirty seconds even when I had a lit one in my mouth, that I talked to people only I could see, that I'd take pieces of fruit and crush them in my hand, that I tried to do Michael Jackson's moonwalk forwards. But to me, everything had seemed completely normal. In other words, everything that had looked crazy to people who hadn't drunk the tea was real and normal to me, until the people watching me convinced me that it was the effect of the tea. It doesn't make you dizzy or queasy or anything. Things are just a bit blurry and you get kinda uncoordinated. But here's the thing: it fucks with your head. You reckon everything's perfectly normal until someone shows you it's not. But this time, up on Canastra Hill, there was no one around to describe the shit I was doing. When I realized, I panicked. The more normal I felt, the more I imagined the absurd, dangerous things I was probably doing, without anyone there to tell me. I was shit-scared. I was afraid I might kill myself without realizing it. I curled up in a fetal position near the tent, determined not to move till morning, till it wore off.'

'Has he got to the part with the dog?'

'Nope. But he's almost there. I'll let you know, Naiara.'

'Now we just have to go round these bushes.'

'I didn't know what to do. I started lighting up one spliff after another and went through the whole brick, hoping it'd calm me down. Made no difference. Could be I'd already smoked it all and was just hallucinating that I still had some. The fire was burning down and I didn't have any more wood. Or maybe there was firewood right under my nose but I thought there wasn't 'cause of the tea. I couldn't be sure of anything.'

'Here we are.'

The six hikers came to a huge rock bulging out of the hillside like scar tissue. It was warm and covered with whitish lichen in several places. Naiara and Isabela sat down first, side by side. Uruguay set his cooler down carefully and sat next to Isabela. Pellet sat a short distance away from the others, but kept looking from one to the next as he talked. Bricky and Hermano remained standing, admiring the view that took in the slick mirror of the Guaíba and much of Porto Alegre's urban sprawl. The cloud cover dramatically reduced the intensity of the colours, like a photograph that hadn't been fully developed. There wasn't a single sliver of blue in the sky.

'I closed my eyes and started to pray for someone or something that could interact with me, tell me how I was acting. I went inside the tent, but instead of feeling protected I freaked out even more. It made me even more aware that I was alone. And, fuck, maybe I wasn't even in the tent. It might've been the tea tricking me. I'd have been happier if someone had appeared out of nowhere and told me I wasn't in the tent, but rolling down the hill with exposed fractures in every limb. That would've been better than being all alone up there *not knowing*.'

'Look. Down there. There's a vulture eating an animal.'

'Where?'

'There.'

'I see it.'

'This is the last beer. Anyone?'

'I've never seen a vulture so close before.'

'Yuck, it's pecking at something really gross.'

'I think it's an opossum.'

'Isabela, scoot a bit closer 'cause I want to tell you something.'

'You can tell me from there, Uruguay. I've got good ears.'

'It's really cool.'

'The air's so still I can't even smell the rotten flesh,' said Hermano, coming over to the others to get a look at the vulture. He sat down next to Naiara.

'Dead animals creep me out,' said Isabela, looking away and making a face.

'You guys ever been to a funeral?' said Bricky, watching the vulture with a lost gaze, as if he were staring at something slightly to one side of it.

No one had.

'I heard a noise outside the tent. It sounded like footsteps. I thought it might be a person, another fuckwit camping on the hill, a boy scout, a ghost, anything. I wasn't afraid. I was way past fear. I needed someone to tell me what I was doing, to be my observer, you know? I stumbled out of the tent and, when I looked, I saw a white dog over by the embers of the fire.'

'Hey, Naiara, he's up to the bit about the dog.'

'A really big white dog, massive. It stood there with its tongue hanging out, looking at me. I wasn't sure if it was a dog, a wolf, some kind of wild animal. I wasn't even sure it was for real, for fuck's sake. Then it lay down, lifted its hind leg and started licking its balls.'

'Any of you ever thought about what you'll be doing in the year 2000?' asked Naiara, ignoring the warning that Pellet had reached the only part of his story that she found funny and still wasn't sick of hearing.

'It didn't stop licking its balls. It just didn't stop.'

'I'll be twenty-four,' said Bricky. 'I'll be in the army. Agulhas Negras Military Academy. Or in the Amazon.'

'I'll be married to Isabela, and I'll ask her to bring me another beer when Faustão starts the countdown to midnight.'

'In your dreams, Uruguay.'

'I reckon Faustão will be dead in the year 2000.'

'Seriously, it licked its balls for an hour. Non-stop. And there was no one around to ask if it was really happening or if I was hallucinating. It's normal for a dog to lick its balls, but not for an hour.'

'I reckon I'll be living somewhere around here,' said Naiara. 'It's not what I want, but it's what I reckon is going to happen. How old will I be? There are nine to go . . .' she said, starting to count on her fingers.

'Twenty-two,' said Hermano.

'Yep . . . twenty-two. It's hard to imagine being that age.'

'Till I couldn't bear it any more. I told myself that if it didn't stop licking its balls, I'd have to kill it. I watched another few minutes of that scene from hell and then I jumped on the dog. And I reckon that's when I blacked out.'

'Maybe I'll be pregnant, or already have a child by then. Or more than one.'

Uruguay whispered something in Isabela's ear. She pulled back and scowled, but a few seconds later she scooted across the rock closer to him.

'Maybe I'll be dead already.'

'Maybe the world'll end in the year 2000. Judgement Day.'

'You're kinda Christian, aren't you, Bricky?'

'My family is.'

'I don't believe we have a soul.'

'You don't have to be Christian to believe in souls, Naiara.'

'I know, but I don't believe in them anyway.'

'Most women believe in souls.'

'I don't.'

'When I woke up on the Sunday morning with the sun hammering my face, I was sprawled on the ground about a hundred yards from the tent. All cut up. It was hard to find a part of my body that *wasn't* covered in mosquito bites. The tent was burned. A huge tear in the side. But at least I found the other half of my cheese.'

'They like tomatoes too. There isn't a woman alive who doesn't like tomatoes.'

'Bricky, the big expert on women.'

'But seriously, Naiara. Do you reckon people just die and that's it?'

'Yep.'

'I don't. I reckon something stays behind when we die. That's the soul. The body dies, but there's a spirit. Like . . . I don't know how to explain. But there's this thing that stays on after our bodies are dead.'

'Doesn't make any difference to me. Death is death.'

The vulture left the mangled carcass, flapped its wings and disappeared over the hill, swooping low. Naiara and Bricky turned to watch it. When she turned back, Naiara looked at Hermano.

'What about you, Hands?'

'So, if anyone here ever decides to have datura tea and needs company, or an *observer*, count on me. I mean it.'

'I reckon you're both wrong. I reckon there's a body and a soul, but it's the soul that disappears when we die, and the body that remains.'

'That's a new one,' said Bricky, looking slightly annoyed.

'How so?' asked Naiara.

None of the three said anything else, not even when Bricky nudged Naiara, who nudged Hermano to show him that Uruguay and Isabela were lying on the lichen kissing, hands timidly parked on each other's inert bodies, statue-like.

6.17 A.M.

Passing under the new Protásio Alves Viaduct, with a structure that looked like it had taken its inspiration from an old-fashioned lunar-landing kit, he imagined that his wife didn't exist, that she had left him or died, a recurrent fantasy that had haunted and seduced him at the most unexpected times ever since Adri had almost died for real, some two and a half years earlier, giving birth to Nara. In a way, it was as if she really had died but insisted on remaining in the world out of sheer stubbornness, overshadowed by a light, never-ending case of post-partum depression. He felt he'd done everything he could to help her recover her former restlessness: paying for cooking classes, buying her presents, and using his connections as a doctor to keep her in a constant supply of free samples of 20mg fluoxetine capsules that came in little boxes with 'Returning the colour to life' written on the back. Although Adri was an affectionate and attentive mother, it seemed as if all her feelings and actions of late were commanded by highly sophisticated automatic-pilot software. She was living as he was driving now, in third gear and cruising at about twenty-five miles an hour, almost completely unaware of what was going on around him, as if the eyes and limbs driving the car were controlled by an operations centre entirely independent of the one responsible for his incessant flow of thoughts. He realized this when a silver Ford Focus sped past, narrowly missing the Montero and accelerating down the new, wide Salvador França Avenue, with its three lanes and central reservation of scrawny palms that the local government had had the gall to call 'urban greening' in its last, unsuccessful campaign for re-election. With the sun imposing itself, he felt annoyed as he remembered that he had suggested several times that they set out earlier, before dawn, to gain time and avoid a few extra hours of driving in the sun, but Renan – who never missed an opportunity to spew rules and remind him that he was the experienced climber and mentor of the expedition – had replied that 'getting up before six is simply unacceptable', a jocular comment that seemed out of keeping with the kind of mental and physical demands they were about to face. The same friend to whom he was going to entrust his very life, the person who had assured him that he could teach him all about ice climbing at base camp

and during the climb itself, thought it was unacceptable to get out of bed two hours earlier to ensure
that the first day of their trip went smoothly. The
contradiction made him so angry that he stepped
on the accelerator, as if wanting to chase the Ford
Focus that had overtaken him. He ignored the red
traffic light in front of the Botanical Garden. Why
hadn't he woken Adri up, even though he knew she
was only pretending to be asleep? In retrospect,
his wife's attitude struck him as a play for attention.
And why hadn't he woken Nara up so he could hear
her little voice before leaving, so he could turn to
stone one last time? It was her favourite game.
Every so often, without warning, he'd pretend to
freeze in the position he was in, as if a spell had
turned him to stone. When she realized her father
had stopped moving, she'd give a little squeal and
start trying everything in her power to restore him
to his human form, with a flurry of shoves, punches,
tickles, jumps and all kinds of attacks, all the while
cackling with laughter and spouting sentences that
showed an impressive vocabulary for a two-and-
a-half-year-old, until he too cracked up laughing
or collapsed or made a brusque movement to indicate that the statue had turned back into her father.
Two and a half. He often mused at length about his
daughter's future, imagining what she'd be like as
a teenager, the accidents she'd have, the dental

problems, sexual discoveries, wondering if she'd see life as a burden or an adventure, and what his role would be in all those experiences. One thing was certain: she took after him in temperament more than she did Adri. She didn't talk a lot, observed everything, and already had a rather adult-like way of suffering in silence that drove Adri to desperation. When she was still in her mother's belly, only his voice had been capable of calming her down when she was agitated: he would usually describe in detail the things they'd do together when she was two, three, five, twelve, eighteen. 'Daddy's going to take you to the place where he grew up, over in the southern suburbs, and we're going to climb a really big hill there, to see the whole city from up high.' 'She's calm now,' Adri would say after about three minutes, fascinated by that precocious interaction between father and daughter. The delivery had been such a traumatic experience that he had unconsciously repressed the memory, but now, with the car speeding along the Terceira Perimetral, the long axis of avenues connecting the city's northern and southern suburbs, he couldn't stop the memories from rushing back, with images flowing from the deepest recesses of his mind, beginning with the realization that Adri's waters had broken and the strange serenity of the moments that followed, both for him and Adri, who, after phoning the obstetrician, had calmly announced that she was going to have a shower and then proceeded to spend a good twenty minutes in there, at least. She had been in high spirits during the drive to the hospital. The obstetrician, Thales, had been his lecturer. He was forty, competent and experienced, although a little too playful for his taste. But Adri liked his wisecracks, and if it made her relax, great. Thales had greeted them with a smile at Moinhos de Vento Hospital and asked, 'Did you manage to contact the father?' Fortunately, in the maternity ward, he went into serious mode and completely stopped messing around when he checked her dilation and decided to put her on oxytocin to induce labour. Thales showed Adri the numerical indicator on the monitoring device and said that with the hormone it would go up to thirty, with peaks of forty, fifty or even a bit more with each contraction. Meanwhile, he tried to pay as little attention as possible to what the obstetrician was doing, trying to put the role of husband before that of doctor, because for some reason it didn't seem right to mix the two. But Adri's pains were growing much stronger, the indicator was going way over fifty, and he was the first to notice that with the peak of each contraction the baby's heartbeat slowed drastically, until it appeared to level out at a much lower rate than normal. He brought it to Thales's attention, at which point all his composure drained away. Adri had developed gestational diabetes in her last month of pregnancy and the diverse complications it could cause during childbirth were beginning to rear their heads. The obstetrician became visibly concerned when he heard that Adri had had a high blood sugar reading the day before, something that he himself, husband-father-doctor, hadn't been aware of, because a few days earlier he had entrusted her with the task of monitoring her own blood sugar levels with a glucose monitor. On the monitor, the baby's heart stopped and started. Adri looked at him, confused, apologizing for not having told him, and his attempt to assess the gravity of the situation and the blame they each deserved for that oversight plunged him into a blinding spiral of self-blame from which he emerged only when he heard Thales requesting an operating room for an urgent C-section. Adri began to cry as she was prepped for surgery, saying she was afraid. He held her hand and told her that everything would be fine, that he'd be there by her side the whole time, when in fact he was afraid too, because despite being a surgeon with a bright career, despite having been considered one of the most brilliant students in the history of his medical school, at that moment he was unable to comprehend what was going on with his wife's and baby's bodies. The part of him that was the doctor ceased to exist, and the only reality was that the lives of the woman he loved and the child still in her belly were in serious danger. The anaesthetist arrived, a very thin woman who appeared to be of Polish descent. She asked the questions that had to be asked and left aside all others, as there wasn't time, and promised Adri that she wouldn't feel any pain, just the movements of the surgical interventions, which shouldn't be confused with pain. He knew, deep down, that the anaesthetist was only saying these things to keep her calm, but it was necessary. The obstetrician and nurses were in a flurry around the operating table. He kissed Adri, told her over and over that he was there, that he'd stay there with her. She was given the epidural, which was supposed to take effect in fifteen or twenty minutes, but to his horror, Thales declared that there wasn't enough time and he'd have to make the incision immediately. Adri's hands were tied. Thales made the first cut and she howled. It was obvious that the anaesthesia still hadn't kicked in. He tried to stroke her face, but she told him not to touch her. With each new intervention by the obstetrician, she howled like a beast being slaughtered, the veins and tendons in her neck bulging, eyes rolling. He suffered his first loss of blood pressure since childhood, so long ago, when he was still overwhelmed by such things. Cloudy vision, shaky hands and legs, cold sweat, nausea. He was about to black out like any first-time father, because he was reduced to precisely that when he saw her face transfigured by a torture he had no way of relieving. He was afraid she might literally die of pain, and there was nothing he could do, because no matter how much he loved her he had no way of sharing the agony with her, shouldering some of the pain. He remembered his mother and the expression on her face whenever he hurt himself as a child, the impossible desire to alleviate her child's suffering. He'd never forgotten that expression. It had taught him from a young age that physical suffering was solitary. He could only witness it, and the sight of his wife's face quickly became unbearable. He got up from his seat beside the operating table and saw, over the top of the curtain that blocked the patient's view, the operation that was taking place. Blood was gushing, neutral and innocent, from the cut in the base of her abdomen. Just as his eyes focused on the scene, the doctor forced the cut open, exposing the layers of skin, fat and flesh in Adri's belly, as distinct as in a textbook diagram, but moist and shiny as only organic matter can be, and there in the middle he could make out the baby's head, covered in blood and amniotic fluid. That was when he regained control and felt the queasiness begin to abate. He couldn't wrap his mind around Adri's unspeakable suffering, but the inside of a human body and the violence of scalpels were familiar territory to a surgeon. It was as if the exposed viscera, contrary to the screams and grimaces of pain, were anonymous. Thales's hands forced the cut open even further and the anaesthetist helped, holding up the ribs, but when he tried to pull the baby out by the head it slipped from his hands as if it had been sucked back into the uterus, which let out a slurp of suction. Adri screamed 'Stop!' with all her might, dragging out the vowel until she had used all the air in her lungs. By now, Thales, the anaesthetist and the nurses were visibly terrified. The baby slipped out of the obstetrician's grasp four times in a row. He was aware that both Adri and the baby could die at any moment and wanted to do something to prevent it, but he didn't know how, nor was there room for another doctor to get involved. He could only be the father, but he didn't know how to be a father yet. The anaesthetist climbed on to the operating table and straddled Adri, using the weight of her body to heave the baby out, a brutal manoeuvre that, in retrospect, took on an almost surreal quality. Remembering it, he was certain that, of the whole episode, this was the moment that had most shocked him. But it worked. Seconds later the baby was in the obstetrician's hands, a tiny being, purple, almost black. And silent. The umbilical cord was cut and the baby whisked away. The obstetrician and the anaesthetist consoled Adri, saying, 'It's over, it's over,' but the doctors, nurses and his wife herself had ceased to exist at that moment, because he was certain his daughter was dead. There was no crying. He stood, catatonic, in a corner of the room for almost two minutes, oblivious to everything, until he finally heard the tiny cry that began as a splutter, then a whine, and finally the shrill, broken cry that was the greatest indication of life, the baby's protest at having been expelled from the cocoon of gestation into the cold, sterile atmosphere of the hospital. Propelled by a new injection of adrenaline, he went to see his daughter. Twenty inches. Seven and a half pounds. A tiny mammal. A minute hunk of living flesh. Everything he had experienced and achieved culminated in that little creature, and everything that happened from that moment until his death would be a mere reflection of the fundamental event taking place at that exact moment. Gripped by this euphoria, he took the baby to its mother. Adri glanced out of the corner of her eye and just moaned, 'Not now.' Only then did he realize that the obstetrician was suturing her belly, she in a state of shock, bearing the torture heroically.

Later, after the baby had been breastfed and family members were gazing at it through the nursery window, he discovered that the entire birth had lasted seven minutes. To him it had felt like seven hours, and weeks later it seemed to have taken an entire day. When he told Adri this, she replied that in her memory it all seemed to have taken place in a matter of seconds. 'To be honest, I remember nothing.' 'What do you mean, nothing?' 'Nothing. I don't remember what happened at the hospital, I don't remember the pain. Nothing. The last thing I remember is the shower I had before leaving home.' As soon as they'd found out the baby's sex Adri had wanted to name her Felícia, but at the last minute, after much insistence, he managed to talk her into the name Nara.

DOWNHILL

The 1990–91 summer break in Porto Alegre's public school system was to last seventy-two days or, more precisely, from 8 December 1990 to 18 February 1991. Intervals between one school year and the next were long enough for it to feel not only as if school had ended, but also that it would never recommence. While the entire city took the opportunity to leave the capital and enjoy some time by the sea, the inhabitants of Esplanada had the eccentric habit of staying home, turning their noses up at the idea of travelling to the coast, or reacting with indifference, convinced that the maddening humidity of Porto Alegre, almost daily barbecues, wetting themselves with the garden hose, and occasional trips to Lami to eat chicken and chips and swim in the hot water were preferable to the traffic jams, high prices, crowds, parties, and treacherous, chocolate-coloured seas on the state's coast, at beaches with grandiose names like Oasis, Casino, Queen of the Sea, Atlantis, Shangri-La. Now that the holidays were almost over, Carnival

loomed as a reminder that the previous year's routine would soon be back. There was tacit permission
to indulge in no-holds-barred revelry anywhere
they wanted from 9 to 12 February, but, even so,
few residents were particularly anxious to explore
much beyond their own streets during Carnival.
Uruguay, Pellet and Chrome Black had filled their
backpacks with underwear, packets of cream-filled
biscuits and sleeping bags and taken the bus to
Laguna, in Santa Catarina – Hell's Door to deprav-
ity. Bricky had gone with his family to their beach
house in Hermenegildo, 'the longest beach in the
world', where, according to him, the biggest attrac-
tions were the Uruguayan beer and the ghost lights
on the sand (he said 'gross lights', which everyone
suspected was incorrect, but no one was sure).
Everyone else stayed in Esplanada, happy to attend
parties at clubs in Belém Novo and watch the samba
parades on TV.

With the fan on high speed just two feet from
his face, Hermano was finally freed from agitated
sleep when his mother opened the door of his room
to announce that lunch was ready. He remembered
dreaming all night long, an unpleasant dream that
was interrupted by brief moments of wakefulness
and then continued where it had left off. He couldn't
remember a single detail of it. Some of his chest
and arm muscles ached. He had stayed up half the

night playing *Metroid*, until he got to the end of the game and discovered that Samus Aran was actually a woman, after which he'd done push-ups, crunches, and curls with his dumb-bells.

After lunch, he got on his bike and rode to Walrus's house. It was four blocks away, one downhill, two uphill and the last one flat. He had retired his old Caloi Cross with the foot brake about a year earlier. Mountain bikes were the thing now, and almost everyone in the neighbourhood had upgraded to the new 26" models, with ten, twelve or fifteen speeds. Hermano's bike was a red, ten-speed Arrojo, which was scoffed at by the owners of Monarks, Calois or imported brands. But he was used to it and, aside from constant glitches in the manual gears, which refused to be adjusted, he liked it. It was heavy and aggressive, made of unusually thick steel tubes. On his way to Walrus's house, as was his habit, he insisted on keeping it in the heaviest gear even during the uphill stretch, each turn of the pedal demanding tremendous effort.

Walrus's house was always undergoing renovation. There was always a wall, balcony or new floor in slow construction. The plaster would split in several places and sometimes it fell, exposing bricks. Now it was the garage that was being expanded, for the second time. Walrus's father had a pot belly, a large moustache and sunburned skin, and spent most of the year in nothing but flip-flops and shorts. On very cold days, he would appear in a black turtleneck pullover. It was always the same one. Not infrequently, the handle of a revolver could be seen in the waistband of his shorts. The extra space in the garage wasn't to make room for another car alongside his black Voyage, but for TV sets, clothing, toys, computers and other items from God knows where, probably stolen cargo. His friends called him, inexplicably, Skinny Face. His contrived friendliness only made him come across as more threatening.

'Come in and put your bike there,' said Walrus when he opened the door, pointing at the garage. Hermano picked his way around two small mounds of gravel and sand and leaned his Arrojo against the garage wall.

When he walked into the living room, Hermano didn't see Walrus, but he did see two Dobermann pinschers. The dogs were standing in the corridor, tense. One of them took a step towards him. Walrus appeared behind them, passed in front of Hermano and said:

'Attack! Attack!'

It wasn't the first time Hermano had come face to face with Armageddon and Predator, but every time the situation repeated itself he couldn't help but feel nervous. The dogs listened to Walrus and backed off, casting Hermano one last threatening look before disappearing down the corridor. Skinny Face had trained his Dobermanns with reverse commands. If someone shouted 'Sit!', 'Lie down!', 'Still!' or 'Amigo!' at the dogs, they would be brutally set upon. 'Attack!', 'Bite!' and the like made them try to put the stumps of their amputated tails between their legs. Hermano followed Walrus up to his room, where he showed him his new computer, which was sitting on a modular desk attached to a beige wardrobe. It looked identical to the last one, with a horizontal case and 14" monitor, but it was a newer model, much more powerful. Skinny Face had a shady business partner who smuggled computers and sold pirate copies of games. Every now and then Walrus would invite a friend or small group over to his place to see the latest game he had copied on a 5¼" floppy disk, or to show them how some new joystick worked. No one else in the neighbourhood had a computer. And if it weren't for the computer, no one would ever have gone to Walrus's house. Every group of growing boys seems to derive a kind of cohesive energy from the cruel segregation of one or more of its members. In Esplanada, the segregated element was Walrus. With the exception of football matches and visits to his house to see his computer games, Walrus was excluded and subject to constant ridicule.

'It's a 386 DX. With thirty-three megahertz and four megabytes of RAM memory.'

'No way.'

'The hard drive's got eighty meg.'

'That's a lot.'

'It holds a *lot* of games. But the best thing is that it's got Super VGA video.'

'Wow.'

'Two hundred and fifty-six colours.'

No matter how fascinated he was by the games and colourful graphics, Hermano couldn't bear to be in Walrus's room for very long. There was an odour that he could only define as the smell of a drooled-on pillowcase. It was mild, perhaps other people wouldn't even notice it, but Hermano started thinking about it before he even entered the room. Driven by the smell, his impatience quickly mounted, and after ten or fifteen minutes all he wanted to do was get out of there. Walrus always had a bottle of Coke with him and would begin to show him the games. It was always the same. Only the games were different. Or sometimes it was a new phase in an old game that he wanted to show him, or the end of a point-and-click adventure that had taken him months to reach. *Golden Axe. Space Quest. Leisure Suit Larry. Maniac Mansion. Heart of China.* Something about him inspired pity, and pity is generally the prelude to contempt. His never-trimmed dark moustache was obscene on his round, pre-adolescent face, with its mixture of adult and childish features. Walrus had never done anything to anyone. He wasn't stupid; he held his own in football. But he suffered from that unfathomable weakness that makes certain people unpopular, the butt of senseless mockery.

After being shown the wonders of the new 386, in an exercise of tolerance that lasted a little over an hour, Hermano said they needed to leave for the downhill championship scheduled for three o'clock at the stairs. Walrus complained that, as usual, he hadn't been told about any championship. Hermano insisted that he come, but he declined, saying he wanted to stay home playing computer games. It was the answer Hermano had been hoping for. As always, as he rode away from Walrus's house, he felt ashamed at the irritation and impatience that had made him almost deaf to the things his friend said and blind to the images on the computer, and he felt the ridiculous urge to go back and apologize, though he didn't really know what for. As always, he just kept pedalling.

Half a dozen kids with their bikes were gathered at the top of the stairs. There were a few more people on the other side of the street, sitting on the low wall that fenced off someone's front lawn. Among them was Bonobo with a girl sitting on his thigh, a blonde who was a stranger to Esplanada, pretty in spite of her crooked teeth. Bonobo merely glanced at Hermano when he slowly crossed the street on his bike and stopped in front of the other cyclists at the top of the stairs. The visual contact was so fleeting and impersonal that it was as if Bonobo hadn't recognized him. Several times after their confrontation on the football pitch, weeks earlier, Hermano had mentally staged a clash with Bonobo, a clash he believed was fated to happen and which, against his will, he imagined in detail several times a day, in moments when he'd rather have been occupied with other thoughts. His imagination worked as if it were projecting a film, cutting from shot to shot of the bloody fight, choreographing every blow and using slow motion for all it was worth.

The stairs were composed of flights of cobbled steps between level areas of beaten earth. They connected two nearby streets, which were almost parallel, but separated by a steep slope. Next to the stairs, flanking the steps, was a wide strip of earth broken up by grass, rocks, holes, and ruts hollowed out by erosion. This was Esplanada's downhill track.

The championships had been inspired by imported magazines about mountain biking and followed a simple and somewhat malleable set of rules:

1. The objective was to descend the strip of beaten earth next to the stairs as fast as possible.
2. It didn't occur to anyone to time each competitor's descent. No one had ever brought it up. It took the elite ten to twelve seconds on average, but the real time was irrelevant. The assessment criteria were how the spectators and other competitors perceived the speed and risk of the ride.
3. In this sense, the riders' frequent spills played a dual role: they could either ruin a descent or be so spectacular that they worked in their favour. A bad fall was pathetic. A good one was glorious.
4. The competitors could attempt the course as many times as they wanted and in any order, as long as everyone was in agreement.
5. The competition ended when a competitor was badly hurt or everyone tired of it and decided to go home, debating who deserved what place.

The street that served as a finish line at the bottom of the stairs wasn't very busy, but it was still a miracle that there hadn't been any deadly collisions with motor vehicles. The most skilled riders managed to stop their bikes with a skid before they got to the kerb, but the manoeuvre came with its own risks.

That afternoon, the competition started out a little more organized than usual. An order was established for the five competitors present. Hermano was fourth. The first was Wagner Montes, riding an imported Trek with semi-automatic gear shifting, a gel saddle and a chrome-molybdenum frame, a light, elegant ride, without a doubt the most expensive and sophisticated in the neighbourhood. Unfortunately, Wagner Montes wasn't a very skilled rider. He actually used his brakes on the way down, which was ridiculous, leaving embarrassing skid marks on the track. His descent this time was, in fact, above average. He didn't brake once, as far as anyone could see, but his average speed was less than impressive. The Joker said that he never *pedalled* during the descent. In short, he was chicken. Next went Pellet, and then Mononucleosis, the group's pet, who, at twelve, appeared to have a promising career in daredevil cycling.

By the time it was Hermano's turn, most people who'd been sitting on the wall had already crossed the street to the top of the stairs to watch the competition. With Bricky, Walrus and other closer friends not present, the audience was made up of people he barely knew: some older cousins of Ingrid's, some kids who lived on streets further away, and some friends of Bonobo's from heaven knows where. When they came over, Hermano overheard a fragment of the story that Bonobo was telling the others. It involved a bottle and shots fired into the air. Bonobo was the protagonist of many such stories. The best known was a kind of founding myth for Bonobo's reputation, and had taken place a little over a year earlier, when his family had just moved to Esplanada. There were many versions, but the general idea was: there used to be a small mulberry tree in the square. It had been planted by old Ijuí, one of the first residents. It was a young tree, about six feet high, with a trunk no thicker than a thumb. That year, its shy top of tiny leaves had been laden with mulberries for the first time. At the request of Ijuí, an old man who was loved by everyone and who planted trees everywhere, the children had all agreed to wait for the mulberries to ripen before picking and sharing them equally. Parents had watched with indulgent, doting faces as their little ones gathered around the mulberry tree hatching mind-boggling theories to predict the day the berries would be ripe. The children had watered the little mulberry tree and invented all kinds of fertilizer for it, using combinations of different-coloured soil, dead insects and fruit peels. Finally, Ijuí had announced that in two or three days, at most, the children would be able to pick the mulberries themselves. On the morning of the third day, when eight children arrived in the square holding straw baskets and plastic bowls to carry out the long-awaited ritual, all they found in the place of the mulberry tree was a sawn-off stump. The atmosphere in the square that morning was one of tears and distress. Ingrid's dad drove past, saw the commotion and stopped the car to say that when he'd gone to buy bread earlier, he'd seen the new residents' son, a delinquent by the name of Bonobo, sawing down the tree and returning home with it on his narrow shoulders, the little black mulberries swinging merrily from its branches. The children's parents had gone to Bonobo's family home. Bonobo himself had answered the door and said yes, he'd taken the tree, so what, street trees don't have owners, if you don't like it, you can try to get it back, but you're going to get hurt, etc. The intimidation had worked, and the parents had gone home resigned and spent the rest of the day consoling their children. A group of older brothers of the traumatized children, however, had felt the community's ire and decided to turn it into physical punishment. Different versions of the story held that between eight and twenty people had surprised Bonobo near a bus stop to teach him a lesson. He had run for a few blocks, then suddenly tired of it, stopped, turned to face his pursuers, grabbed a rock with one hand and a heavy piece of wood with the other, and said, 'Bring it on.' He'd beaten them all and managed to get away. A convoy of two cars had taken the injured to the emergency room. A little over a year later, few of those involved were willing to talk about it, and some had even moved away. They had fuzzy memories of that piece of wood swinging, those fantastically short arms delivering blows with animal fury. The fact is that Bonobo had beaten up eight of them. Or fifteen. Or twenty, according to the most exaggerated versions. Bonobo himself loved to confirm the story, but referred to it with calculated contempt, as if it were the sort of thing that happened all the time (and it was, in a way). He claimed that his front tooth, broken in half, was a trophy of that fight.

As he got ready to ride, Hermano felt Bonobo's eyes boring into the back of his neck. He placed his hands firmly on the rubber grips of the handlebars. Only his middle fingers remained outstretched, resting on the handbrakes. It was a quirk of his to brake using his middle fingers instead of his index fingers. He pedalled a few times to push off and picked up speed on the slope. Pedals aligned at the same height, knees and elbows slightly bent. He pedalled two more times to reach maximum speed. The cobbled steps flew past on his left. Halfway down there was a hump in the terrain, and from there on the slope was even steeper, reaching approximately forty-five degrees, and then tapering off on the home straight. Hermano jumped over the hump. Back at the top of the stairs, someone honoured the stunt with an enthusiastic shout. He was good at it. He was the best. He almost always won. And his falls were highly spectacular. He knew that over a certain speed it was virtually impossible to maintain control of the bike. And what interested him most was passing this limit, entering the zone in which brakes were useless and the bike appeared to glide on a wire. The possibility of a terrible accident was left to chance. He reached the end of the track, where the already much milder slope gave way to a horizontal stretch. He stopped on the beaten earth with a precise skid. It had been a good ride, certainly one of his personal best times.

As he climbed the stairs with his bike on his shoulder, he saw the Joker position himself at the top of the hill and begin his descent. He flew past him, pedalling hard. The Joker was Hermano's only rival in downhill racing. Hermano didn't stop to look back to watch his adversary's performance and kept walking, with a nonchalance that was a part of the whole *mise en scène*. Besides, his attention was trained on the top of the stairs, where Bonobo and his thuggish-looking pals were gathered. When he got to the top, Wagner Montes complimented him on his excellent ride, but no one else said a thing or even looked at Hermano. He suddenly felt very alone. He wasn't close to any of those people. There were two or three conversations going on, but he couldn't really work out what they were about. He saw Naiara arriving with Isabela. Isabela was wearing red lipstick. Hermano thought her make-up was vulgar, horrible. Naiara was barefoot, her dirty little feet treading the cobblestones without a care. The features she shared with her brother were only evident if you looked for them. Slightly upturned nostrils, lips almost the same beige colour as their skin. Simian features, reminiscent of illustrations of their hominoid ancestors. He thought about striking up a conversation with the girls, but in the presence of Bonobo he and Naiara never spoke. He didn't know why. They barely greeted each other. Bonobo was now entwined with the blonde with the crooked teeth. Hermano thought about leaving. He thought about heading back to Walrus's house and telling him that he was the only decent person in the neighbourhood. Only Walrus deserved his respect. With him he didn't even have to talk. They could sit around staring at computer games and drinking Coke in mammoth-sized green glasses, and the minutes passed one after another and made sense. Walrus was the wise one, at home playing on his computer.

The Joker came climbing the stairs with a monstrous grin cutting his pimply face in half. Hermano hadn't seen his descent, but the smile said it all. He soon saw that the general consensus was that the Joker had been the best so far.

Hermano asked to ride again right after the Joker, disrupting the prearranged order. The challenge was implicit. Authorization was granted.

Instead of positioning himself at the top of the stairs, the official start line, Hermano leaned his bike against a post and started to pace the pavement, looking for something on the ground. He found a few abandoned bricks in the grass. Mononucleosis asked what he was doing, if he was going to go or not. Hermano didn't answer. He just placed the bricks on the kerb, creating a small step between the street and the pavement. One by one, the conversations all stopped and people turned to watch Hermano. He asked two of Bonobo's friends to move off the top of the stairs. Bonobo had stopped kissing the blonde and was watching too. When Hermano began pushing his bike up the street, his intention became clear to those watching. 'This ain't going to end well,' muttered the Joker under his breath. Hermano walked about fifty yards uphill, stopped, got on his bike and began to pedal as hard as he could towards the stairs. As he passed Bonobo, he looked him right in the eye. Now he was paying attention. Now Bonobo would see. He used the brick step to help him on to the pavement and when he launched into his descent he was already travelling at a high speed. He continued pedalling with all his might. No one would ever ride that track as fast as he was riding it now. It was impossible. He felt as if his wheels weren't even touching the ground. The world around him became a blur and the wind made his eyes water. In the first few seconds, he realized the bike was already out of his control. But even so he kept pedalling harder and harder. He knew he was going to fall. And everyone was going to see him fall. On the way down, he understood that the only thing motivating him to ride that track so many times was the possibility of a fall, the chance he might really hurt himself. And this would be the most spectacular of all falls. It was what he had to say to the people at the top of the stairs. He was ready to bleed. It was his talent. If Bonobo was capable of beating up twenty people at once, now he was capable of cutting, breaking, grazing, flaying, scraping, fracturing, scratching, perforating and crushing his own body in a way that no one would ever forget. As he rode over the hump halfway down, Hermano pulled up on the handlebars, launching the bike into the air. He landed fifty yards down. The force of the impact made the handlebars swivel all the way to the right and the bike was thrown to the left, landing on the stone steps. Cyclist and bike went tumbling down the stairs. There was no pain, just the feeling of being completely out of control, which brought more resignation than panic. His body was battered in turns by stone steps, steel tubes and rubber tyres. It was almost like catching a wave, body surfing. All he could think of was a scene from a movie: the last of the V8 interceptors rolling in the apocalyptic desert, bouncing and spinning as if in an Olympic gymnastics solo, projecting sheets of sand against the light-blue sky, and seconds later the road warrior emerges from the wreck with a bloody face, a terrible eye injury and a wounded arm, and drags himself out of the car and over the scalding sand, which sticks to his blood, to his open wounds, and the murderous motorcycle gang races down the hill towards him to see if he's still alive, and he is, seriously injured and covered in blood and abandoned, but you can see him and imagine yourself in his place. When his own body stopped rolling, Hermano raised his hands to his face, then pulled them back and there he was, in the broad palms of his hands, in his thick, strong fingers. People were running down the stairs towards him. His enemies racing down the hill to see if he was still alive. Spectators running to save the hero of the movie. His movie. The scene was perfect. The make-up couldn't have been more realistic. Blood is such a beautiful thing, he thought before he blacked out.

Samara was stroking her son's forehead with the tips of her fingers. It was only nine o'clock at night and he told her he wanted to sleep but was finding it hard, because during the holidays he was used to going to bed after midnight and it was still too early. He wasn't sleepy, but he wanted to sleep. A small part of his scalp, near his forehead, had been shaved and was sporting a bandage. There were several pretty ugly scrapes and scratches on his body too, some Mercurochrome-orange, and his wrist was broken. Samara was certain that her son was in pain and wanted to stop him from feeling it, but he swore that he could hardly feel a thing and that he was fine, all he wanted to do was go to sleep and wake up the next morning. She thought about mentioning the red spots she'd found in the bathroom, but sensed that they had their origin in something her son didn't want to talk about. She didn't feel close enough to him to broach the subject. She gave up trying to fathom out his feelings and secret actions and decided to focus on the sleep problem. Perhaps that was something she could solve.

'Remember how I used to make you sleep when you were younger?'

Hermano remembered. His mother's fingers on his forehead felt really nice. His injuries itched more than they hurt.

'Imagine you're climbing some stairs, very slowly.' Samara spoke languidly, stretching out each word, as if she herself were sleepy.

Before closing his eyes, Hermano took a good look at his mother. When he closed them, he put himself in her place, imagining that he was the woman sitting on the edge of the bed, observing her son. It began as a quick, involuntary exercise of the imagination, then he realized he was unable to exit her point of view.

'And at the top of the stairs . . . there is . . . a cloud . . .'

He felt, or at least thought he could feel, exactly what she was feeling as she tucked into bed, like a child, her fifteen-year-old son, who'd suffered an ugly bike accident that afternoon and had blacked out and been carried home by his friends and taken to the emergency room, where his wrist had been bandaged and he'd received two external and two internal stitches in his head, where there was a cut so deep the doctor had said he could see his skull.

'A lovely soft white cloud . . . you want to sink into it.'

He remembered all the other times she had made him fall asleep like that, when he was afraid to go to sleep because he couldn't stop thinking there was a zombie lurking somewhere in his room, in the dark, every night, even when he told himself there was no such thing as zombies and that his fear was ridiculous. The zombie had a crazy face, smiled with bulging eyes and babbled that it was hungry for brains, like in a movie he'd seen on videotape when he was seven or eight years old, with Bricky, who at the time was better known as Túlio. He thought about all the time his mother, and his father too, had devoted to him over the years. The enormity of the investment. He saw it all at once, the whole fifteen years of money and time and attention and sacrifice that his parents had dedicated to him. It was such a strange thing to imagine.

'You climb on to the cloud . . . make yourself comfortable, nice and cosy. It smells like fabric softener . . .'

There was his mother's voice, repeating the technique she had used when he was a child to bring on sleep, but it wasn't working. He wasn't growing sleepy; in fact he was feeling more and more awake, his mind increasingly agitated.

'Your eyes are growing heavy . . . your body's really relaxed, you're sinking into the cloud . . .'

He wanted to get up and go out to find his friends and talk about the fall, about what had happened at the emergency room. To be the centre of attention for a few minutes. But with his newly acquired ability to put himself in his mother's shoes, he imagined how frustrating it would be for her if he told her he didn't feel like sleeping any more and, in fact, wanted to go out. Then he imagined what she would feel if he really did fall asleep.

'And on this cloud is the word . . .'

He wanted her to feel what he imagined she would feel.

'*Sleep . . .*'

He pretended to be asleep.

6.23 A.M.

His daughter's name made him realize where, in fact, he was driving. For the first time, he felt comfortable enough to admit to himself that he didn't like the name. He thought it was ugly – the very name he had practically forced his wife to accept, after much insistence and fictitious justifications. 'Nara,' he said out loud, and the sound of the word sent a vibration running through a membrane in his mind that held a dense concentration of unfulfilled possibilities, set aside for one reason or another in favour of others that had come to fruition. The name evoked a diffuse, not entirely pleasant feeling of nostalgia, which he felt he had entered physically as he left the last repaved stretch of Aparício Borges Avenue, which became Teresópolis Avenue, which was still undergoing roadworks for a few hundred yards until it gave way to a scenario that looked preserved, with the same old-fashioned tarmac and central reservations with enormous trees that he had seen frequently until some five years earlier, when he still lived in the southern suburbs and often drove that way. He fantasized that the interminable thoroughfare was chasing him and he was now racing it in his car, as he had already raced cloud shadows on highways. Like a pyroclastic flow, the concrete of the new avenues feeding into the Terceira Perimetral advanced like a giant wave engulfing the tarmac, pavements, trees, bus stops and vehicles behind him, and he had to step on the accelerator and get to Esplanada before it was too late. If the concrete caught up with him, he too would turn to concrete, and this time it would make no difference if Nara squealed and tickled him, he would be forever imprisoned in that monochromatic landscape, like the plaster cast of a victim of Pompeii, or Han Solo in the opening sequence of *The Return of the Jedi*. Teresópolis Avenue quickly became Nonoai Avenue, which became Eduardo Prado Avenue, a still-dormant stretch on which the urban sprawl of the last five years had left a variety of marks, though all relatively superficial. Decadent motels, food carts announcing bacon-and-cheese specials, and a few plots of vacant land gave way to small supermarkets, low-income housing, and Assembly of God churches with enormous signs exclaiming 'Stop Suffering!', although their doors were closed at six-thirty on a Saturday morning, an hour at which, it appeared, few people suffered.

When the road began to climb, he anticipated the roundabout a quarter of a mile uphill, where he'd have to take a left on the narrow paved road to the semi-rural district of Vila Nova, where, on a small property surrounded by peach plantations, Renan was probably just waking up after a night of good-bye sex with Keyla, which he would describe over the course of the day in excessive detail. It was an awful habit of Renan's. Once, during a night training session at Condor, he had swung up to grab the last hold of a difficult route on the negative wall. His hand had touched the hold, but he'd forgotten to use magnesium and his sweaty hand had slipped. Renan, who was responsible for safety, should have been paying attention to what was going on, but was instead recounting in gynaecological detail his favourite student, whom he'd finally laid, and was a split second late engaging the belay device. He'd narrowly escaped a trip straight to Intensive Care with a crushed face. Even worse was that Renan had showed no sign of recognizing his imprudence. They were partners, but they couldn't have been more different climbers. Renan had already been second in the Brazilian ranking. He was the co-ordinator of the Technical Commission of the Rio Grande do Sul Mountain Climbing Association. A professional climber. But there was something dis-agreeable about the way he related to the sport, always seeking little victories and achievements, obsessed with the degree of difficulty of each climb he undertook, on a constant quest for the best time, the first 10b route in Brazil's south, the first 100 per cent natural climb on this or that rock, the first to 'do' each new female student that came to the Condor for a few trial lessons, and now his dream was to be the first to climb Cerro Bonete in the Bolivian Andes. Even his friend's physique was somewhat presumptuous and vulgar, with his angular, bulging muscles, his body devoid of fat, his triangular face ending in a pointy chin. It was vanity that took Renan to the top, but there was a brutal contradiction between excessive vanity and a sport like climbing. Contrary to Renan, he considered climbing first and foremost a kind of meditation, an exercise in self-knowledge extended to each of the body's two hundred and twelve muscles. It wasn't strength or impulsiveness that made someone climb a rock, it was a much more delicate wisdom, a complex economy of muscular effort and balance, a dance of contraction and repose led by a mind that was focused and disconnected from everything that was not body or rock. He flipped on the indicator several yards before the roundabout, but when he got to the turn-off to Renan's house he drove straight past it. Instead, he turned off the indicator and stayed on Eduardo Prado. He was pissed off at Renan, but he felt suddenly certain that his own relationship to climbing was also far from ideal. While Renan was motivated by vanity, for him it was an escape. He wanted to believe it was only for the physical and mental conditioning, for the contact with nature that rock climbing fostered, but in reality he was running away. He climbed because deep down he admired Renan. He admired Renan because Renan was everything he wasn't. And now he saw that he had bought into the idea of the expedition to Cerro Bonete because the summit of Cerro Bonete would always be the opposite of where he was now. In 1923, when George Mallory was asked why he wanted to climb Mount Everest, his reply was: 'Because it's there.' His own motivation was the opposite. He didn't want to climb Bonete because the mountain was there, but because he was here. Renan wanted to be able to brag and sell the photographs to a magazine when they got back. Escapism and vanity. There had never been a more misguided pair of climbers. And by not turning left at the roundabout, continuing on and passing in front of the old SinSation Show Club towards the neighbourhood he'd left five years earlier, he believed he was beginning to set things right. The colossal eighty-litre camping backpack rolling again in the boot was a useless burden. 'Go ahead and sleep,' he said out loud, as if Renan could hear him. 'Stay in bed till eleven, which is a much more acceptable hour, isn't it?' After passing over two consecutive electronic road bumps under the speed limit, he let the Montero cruise down a long, serene slope. The silence began to bother him for the first time since he'd left home. He turned on the sound system, unable to remember what CD was in it. He immediately recognized Elomar's guitar, followed by his voice. *From far away on the great journey, overburdened I stop to rest.* He suddenly remembered his dream from the night before, after hours of tossing and turning, unable to get to sleep: he was driving his car in fast-moving traffic on a busy avenue. Beside him, in the passenger seat, was Adri. In the back were Renan and Walrus, a childhood friend he hadn't seen for some fifteen years and whom he had no reason to remember, not even in a dream. The traffic was annoying him. The others were silent. It wasn't clear where they were going. There was a bang, and in the rear-view mirror he saw black smoke billowing from his back tyre. He was forced to pull over to see what had happened. Everyone got out and they stood there a while, staring at the tyre, unable to comprehend what kind of mechanical flaw might have caused it. The landscape stretching away from the avenue was like the sort that runs alongside country highways, a sloping landfill giving way to a vast tract of swampy land. He was distracted by the landscape for a moment, until he heard the drone of the Montero's engine: someone had stolen the car while no one was looking. He barely had time to think about what to do when another vehicle, an older saloon that might have been a Del Rey or a Monza, pulled over and offered them a lift to a police station or something like that. They climbed in, Renan in front, Adri, Walrus and himself in the back, while the driver, who had no striking physical features, drove in silence. When they reached their destination, it wasn't a police station, but a simple house in a working-class neighbourhood, with plaster eczema peering through the worn white paint and a raggedy little lawn out front. Thinking they'd been kidnapped, they obeyed the driver's instructions and went inside, where they found themselves in a large living room with thirty or forty people in it, men, women and children. Some were standing, but most were sitting on brown imitation-leather sofas or on the floor, on fluffy rugs, in circles or half circles. At least half a dozen of those present were wearing identical navy-blue T-shirts, without patterns or brand names, all oversized, as if someone had mistakenly ordered extra-large. It was obvious from the outset that these uniformed individuals were monitors or organizers of some sort, moving

people from place to place, looking around, coord-
inating games, and giving talks to small groups of
attentive listeners. The driver came and handed
them some pamphlets whose content made it clear
that the activities taking place belonged to a strange
school of self-help with religious overtones. They
felt awkward mingling and taking part in the activities, but it was clear to them that the whole thing
wasn't just bait, but also a façade for something
menacing. He tried to convince Renan that they
should do something, and Adri began to protest
and attack the monitors and students with sarcastic
remarks. Renan was sucked in and joined one of
the study groups on some sofas. By now, Walrus
had disappeared. He was afraid to defy the monitors, but Adri opposed them openly, which
heightened the tension in the house. The monitors
exchanged serious looks, as if planning to take
some kind of drastic action. He called Adri over
and whispered in her ear, explaining that it was
better to go along with things and pretend to be
participating in that circus, because they could be
in serious danger if they didn't. She agreed and
they sat on some armchairs, observing what was
going on around them. The monitors' speech was
extremely artificial. The fact that they weren't what
they appeared to be, that they in fact had a much
more sinister agenda than offering life lessons and

religious teachings to all those people, was evident to the two of them and no one else. His teeth seemed to be pressing on one another in his mouth, as if he were grinding them, or as if his wisdom teeth were crowding his other teeth with abnormal force. He opened his mouth wide, and his jaws popped, but the discomfort remained. He began to recognize some of the people in the room. He saw Keyla, some fellow climbers from Condor, and a few patients he'd seen or operated on in the last three years. He saw Jade, a seventeen-year-old girl whose breasts he'd augmented with 275cc implants, despite his insistence that it was totally unnecessary in a young woman with such a lovely, harmonious body, and he also recognized Liliana Caliope, largely responsible for establishing his precocious reputation as a miracle-worker, an equine 52-year-old socialite who swore to anyone who would listen that she had been reborn after his advanced surgical interventions, and who had tried for months to compensate him for his services with much warmer, more intimate payments than those from her inexhaustible bank balance. And only then, scanning the room for more familiar faces, did he notice that there were TV sets everywhere, on tables and in wall cabinets. He was pretty sure they hadn't been there before and that they'd been surreptitiously installed by the monitors. They were large

flat-screen TVs, about thirty-three inches. The
screens suddenly lit up, but instead of a programme
or a grainy screen indicating a lack of signal, they
gave off an intense white light that pulsed slightly,
casting a phantasmagorical luminescence over
people and furniture. Slowly, calmly, everyone
present, except the monitors, began to flock around
the TV sets. He instinctively knew he had to stay
away from them at all costs, as they represented an
indescribable threat. The pressure of his teeth in
his mouth was growing stronger and more painful.
He lost sight of Adri, but his fear of the TVs
trumped any other concern. He crouched behind
sofas and tried to slip away unnoticed through a
series of corridors and recesses, but he kept coming
across more and more TV sets, and a long, terrify-
ing part of the dream was taken up with his
interminable escape until he entered a room and
saw yet another glowing screen with a small group
huddled around it. Suddenly it flashed and the faces
of the people in front of it disappeared. They were
replaced with smooth, black, expressionless surfaces. The same thing began to happen to all the
TVs and the people around them, the same flash
and the same defacement. He tried to get away,
trying to keep a distance from all the TVs, but he
was blinded by a flash that came out of nowhere.
When he opened his eyes again, dazed, he realized

he was somewhere else. The ground was hard, and the panoramic view took in faraway fields and hills. He was standing on a bare, slippery rock, moistened by recent rain. He recognized the place when he saw a large white cross at one end of the rock. He was on top of Cruz Rock, in the company of dozens of other people, everyone who had been at the house of TVs and many more. The people were more or less organized in a long queue, and after rubbing his eyes and looking more closely, he could see they were all mutilated or injured in some way. There were men with missing limbs, fat women with multiple stab wounds in their backs, people riddled with bullets, pieces of flesh hanging from their bodies, disfigured, burned. The queue moved slowly towards one edge of the boulder. When they got there, monitors in the same navy-blue T-shirts strapped each person into a rappel seat, attached a figure eight and passed a rope through it. One by one, they turned and took careful steps backwards into the void, beginning a descent down a bottomless cliff face. Renan was among them, his left femur exposed. The driver who had picked them up from the side of the road reappeared in front of him. When he went to speak to the man, it felt as if his mouth were full of loose teeth. He started spitting them out, first one by one, then the molars and premolars and canines and incisors all came out together in a syrup of crystalline saliva that contained no traces of blood. He ran his tongue over his gums and felt the holes left by his teeth, sensitive but not painful. The pressure was gone, his jaw felt loose and flexible, and the cold air in his mouth brought a sense of relief. Free of his teeth, he began to understand what was going on. 'How did it happen?' he asked the driver, who was still standing next to him. 'A fall. About six hundred feet. Problem with the rope.' 'Thanks,' he said, and headed to the cliff, where he joined the mutilated crowd. The dream finished there. He hadn't remembered a dream in such detail for a long time. He didn't feel a need to interpret it. If someone had asked him at that moment what it meant, he wouldn't have been able to answer, but he knew that its meaning had already been incorporated into his awareness, diluted in his flow of thought. Now a single detail caught his attention. What had Walrus been doing in the dream? He hadn't thought about him for years; never had a truly memorable experience with him. Just then, he remembered that it actually hadn't been fifteen years since he'd last seen Walrus. He'd run into him once, about three or four years earlier. Where had it been? At a restaurant. That was right. At a popular pizza parlour. Back then he couldn't afford to splurge on expensive restaurants, but every now and then he'd be dragged to a place like that by friends. He'd gone to the till to pay and there had been a fat guy in front of him. It had taken him a moment to recognize Wallace Wissler. His childhood friend was wearing a real leather jacket that smelled new, jeans and yellow trainers. His face was still spherical, though slightly longer, and the rat's moustache and sparse beard of the old days had become a straight-lined goatee the exact width of his chin. They had talked for two minutes. Walrus had started out as a trainee with a small web design company in the mid nineties. Just over a year later he'd started his own business with a friend. He'd begun designing basic three-page websites for clients such as bakeries, video rental shops and distributors of orthopaedic supplies, and his company, Stunt, was now responsible for the webpages of a bank, a telecommunications giant and an impressive portfolio of multinationals, celebrities, political parties and institutions. He was accompanied by his wife, a blonde who would never need plastic surgery in her life. In their two-minute conversation, Walrus asked if he was still in touch with other friends from Esplanada, and mentioned a few absurd-sounding nicknames. As he left the pizza parlour, he saw Walrus turning off the alarm of the latest model BMW estate. That was the last time he'd seen him. Nevertheless, his presence in the dream was odd.

On the other hand, it made sense, a lot of sense. After all, it was to the stamping ground of his youth that he was driving now, taking a left on Juca Batista. *Oh new moon, would that I could see her, at the dawn of it all, in the lost era, on a highway morn, and start all over.* Elomar's song was nearing the end, and he was nearing Esplanada.

ISABELA'S FIFTEENTH
BIRTHDAY PARTY

A few minutes to four that Saturday morning, Hermano and Bonobo were walking quickly down the pavement of Shade Street towards Serraria Road, side by side. Hermano, dressed in baggy dark-blue jeans, his dad's brown leather shoes and a salmon-coloured polo shirt, had four fingers of each hand wedged in his pockets with his thumbs hanging out. Bonobo was wearing a tragicomic combination of M2000 Propulsion trainers with pyramidal shock absorption, black Tactel trousers, a beaten-up tweed sports jacket over a white Suicidal Tendencies T-shirt, and a grubby orange cap on his shaved head. They made no noise except for the soles of their shoes on the wet, sandy pavement. A light rain had been falling until about half an hour earlier. Block after block, the street transformed, with gentle curves this way and that and a slope that grew progressively steeper. An abundance of weeds pushed up through cracks in the cobblestones. The street seemed to be slowly

winding its way into the depths of a forest per-
fumed by imposing cedars, which stood, some
sixty feet tall, on both sides. Water slid down their
viscous black trunks, which were covered in para-
sitic tufts of mistletoe, and the treetops grew higher
and denser, knitting together until they formed a
dome of branches and leaves overhead.

Bonobo took a packet of cigarettes out of his
pocket, pulled one out and accidentally dropped it.
Hermano stopped as Bonobo stooped to pick it up.
It was a little wet, but he put it in his mouth and lit
it anyway. For an instant they looked at each other
as if trying to remember something they wanted
to say, but said nothing. Bonobo held out the packet
to Hermano.

'No, thanks.'

At each new intersection there was at least one
Umbanda offering. There were dead black chickens, bottles of cachaça, bowls of popcorn,
snuffed-out candles, flowers and red ribbons, all
strewn about and made soggy by the rain. At the
last intersection before Serraria Road, Bonobo
went over to an offering, took a bottle of 7 Campos
de Piracicaba cachaça, and checked to see if the lid
was still sealed. He returned to the pavement with
the bottle and kept walking beside Hermano. Bonobo's lips were split and swollen, the top one
resembling a disgusting chunk of roast sausage.

The filter of the cigarette dangling from his mouth became tinged with red. He opened the bottle, took the cigarette out of his mouth and had a swig. He pointed the bottle at Hermano, who refused again, not only because he was tenaciously abstinent, but also because he felt that drinking stolen booze from a black-magic offering wasn't something you should do without batting an eyelid, no matter how much of an unbeliever you were. He waited for Bonobo to call him a faggot or the like, but the silence continued. They kept walking with their heads down and eyes glued to the pavement, Hermano with his enormous hands in his pockets, Bonobo puffing on his cigarette between swigs of the cachaça he'd stolen from the *orixás*. The dome of organic matter began to thin out as they approached the corner of Serraria Road, once again exposing the black sky devoid of clouds and stars. A few cars sped along the shiny tarmac – drunk drivers trying to get home as quickly as possible to avoid falling asleep at the wheel. To Hermano, just walking home at that hour, that damp, dismal night, made him feel vaguely in the wrong. Bonobo didn't seem to have any recollection of the incident in the football match during the summer break. Hermano didn't mention it and the corners of his mouth curved into a sad smile when he thought about how differently it had affected each of them.

He was alert to every sound and movement made by Bonobo, who was slowly ceasing to be a threat, an adversary. They were just walking along in the middle of the night and that was it. Hermano was secretly elated by his improbable companion. The night was ending well.

'What a shit party,' said Bonobo, breaking the silence.

'Tell me 'bout it.'

Isabela's fifteenth birthday party had mobilized Esplanada's youth. It had been held at the Recanto Espanhol Restaurant, in Guarujá, the next neighbourhood over. The words SMART CASUAL ATTIRE on the invitation had given rise to considerable debate and many jokes among the male guests in the week leading up to it, but threats to show up in flip-flops and tank tops hadn't been acted on, and most had managed to rustle up at least a blazer and tie so as not to offend the hosts.

From 9 p.m., presents and flowers began piling up on a table by the door while the soundtrack of the soap opera *Vamp* played over the sound system. Half of the tables had been removed, dividing the restaurant into two, an area for dining and another for dancing. The cream used in the chicken fricassée had clearly been watered down, the potato straws were gone in about three minutes, the onion in the salad had had all the flavour scalded out of it, and the white rice was, well, white rice. The potato salad, at least, was abundant and tasty, and the grape *sagu* for dessert wasn't half bad, with just the right hint of wine. The girls strutted around in lipstick and tight dresses, gyrating and waving their arms to the sound of Lenny Kravitz, retreating to the edge of the dance floor during a Chris Isaak ballad, chewing their nails without a worry about their nail polish and gossiping in whispers. After dinner a video montage of scenes from Isabela's childhood was projected on to a wall. The photos and small clips of home videos were captioned: 'Fourth birthday party – 1980' (a children's party with aunties in 'mum' shorts, uncles in moustaches and very short nylon shorts, and a party entertainer dressed as a clown hugging a smiling mini-Isabela), 'Summer in Passo de Torres – 1982' (little Isabela in a bathing suit standing between tents on a campsite holding a supposedly freshly caught kingfish), 'Silver Medal in Swimming at the Professor Gaúcho Club – 1988' (in a bathing suit on the podium, goggle-marks around her eyes, unsure what to do with the arms and legs that had grown too quickly), 'Elementary School Graduation – 1990' (scroll, black gown, among friends), etc. After each section of the video, there was applause, whistling and wisecracks. Afterwards, Isabela danced a waltz with her father. Her heavy foundation ran down her face as she perspired, her light-blue satin dress clung to her plump body, and Uruguay nudged the others at his table and whispered, 'I got it on with her.' Modest amounts of beer were served in plastic cups by three waiters. Hermano drank one soft drink after another and started making disgusting spit bubbles every time the guy in black with the pony-tail and VHS camera on his shoulder passed their table. This on-camera rebellion was part of a pact between him, Bricky, Pellet, Uruguay, the Joker and others, designed to sabotage the family video of the party with a kind of poetic terrorism. Uruguay and the Joker were pretending to be a couple, holding hands and stroking each other's faces whenever the video-maker's lens came near them, while Bricky did his famous imitation of Dr Strangelove, his left hand trying to stop his right arm from making the Nazi salute, shouting 'Heil Hitler!', 'Lufthansa!', 'Volkswagen!' and other senseless things that sounded German. Behind their mocking behaviour and references to the tackiness of the ceremony, however, they were trying to hide the fact that they were a little moved, secretly enjoying an authentic rite of passage, which surfaced in brief collective silences. Between one joke and another, Bricky drifted off into a reverie. Sitting beside him, Hermano saw in his friend's eyes the strange recognition that time was already passing.

By eleven o'clock, most of the half-drunk adults and extended family had gone home or retired to quieter parts of the restaurant. Only Isabela's mother, a woman with indigenous features and long, straight black hair like her daughter's, dressed in a pink skirt suit with purl edges, was still circulating among the birthday girl's friends, who were proving to be rather precocious and insatiable drinkers – inhabitants of a reality that was increasingly unfathomable to her. She finally plonked herself down at a table in the part of the restaurant where dinner had been served, now a dark cemetery of empty tables on which cream-streaked plates, plastic cups with nibbled edges, dying candles capsizing in bowls of water, and messy tablecloths lay like dead flowers on graves. She lit a cigarette, crossed her legs, folded her arms with the cigarette-holding hand just beneath her face and sat there in the most feminine of poses, exhaling smoke and staring with a vaguely perplexed expression at the other half of the room, where some thirty teenagers including her daughter were dancing to absurdly aggressive-sounding music, not in pairs, but alone, transformed into robotic silhouettes by the strobe lights.

Amidst the jumping crowd, one head projected itself above the others, shaking and turning around on an impossible axis. With his eyes closed, banging into shoulders, elbows, chests and hips, stepping on feet and being stepped on in turn, Hermano could taste the lack of oxygen in his throat. The pleasure of wasting energy was the redemption, his reward for enduring a series of conversations and rituals with a spirit of tolerance. Between one song and the next, a brief pause to let sweat drip, relieve dizziness, apologize for a violent elbowing that wasn't intended to hurt, exchange animal-like cries and goofy smiles. Then more walls of distortion over spectres of melody, kick drums pummelled at the speed of light by double pedals, knees and necks waltzing with the magnificent brutality of the music. He was dancing, and loved everyone who was dancing with him. The climax of all that staged aggressiveness was an extreme kind of tenderness. All he had to do was jump higher and higher, and shake his head and arms ever more explosively, until he completely lost his senses, the abolition of all thought, bodies united by exhaustion, sheer happiness, heart failure.

Until 'Patience' began to play. Hermano backed away, disgusted. The girls who had kept their distance until now flocked to the dance floor. Pairs formed, a few people staggered about alone, yet others gave up dancing and went for a drink outside, where the gusts of cold wind would soon give way to light rain. Hermano sat on a chair beside a nearby table. Instead of the peace of endorphins, the only residue of his effort was sweat and tiredness. His neck insisted on drooping forward. Isabela had her arms wrapped around Uruguay, who looked like he was stooped over her, hands attached to her backside, trying to keep as much of their bodies in direct contact as possible. They turned on the dance floor with excruciating slowness. When Uruguay's face became visible, Hermano saw his friend's solid jaw resting on Isabela's trapezius muscle, eyes closed, long hair clinging to the side of his face. At first sight he looked like a man in love, but this impression soon gave way to another, of clumsy, exaggerated effort, as if he were holding Isabela forcefully, so she couldn't get away, a subtle form of coercion. There was something sinister about it. Between Pellet and Lara, on the other hand, there was a giant space, like a crevasse in a glacier. You couldn't have said that his right hand was holding her left hand, exactly, as they were barely touching. Pellet was talking non-stop and chubby-cheeked Lara, with her curly blonde hair and green eyes, in a bold little black dress that made her look older and emphasized the contour of her spine, uninterested in the irreversible effects of datura tea on the human psyche, gazed over his shoulder with the stare of a very old person receiving an intramuscular injection in the arm at a public health clinic, the ultimate empty stare. The Joker and Chrome Black were standing in the middle of the dance floor, whispering. The topic of their conversation was obviously Naiara and Corina, who were making their way around the dance floor in a discreet search for male company. Corina was one of the neighbourhood girls who was already sexually active. The Joker was staring at the two of them with a serious expression, lips pressed together in deep thought, then suddenly he turned to his companion, flashed his trademark grin and mumbled something that made Chrome Black nod in agreement. Nevertheless, they showed no sign of leaving the dance floor to talk to the girls or do anything else. Bricky was dancing with a girl from another neighbourhood, perhaps one of Isabela's school friends. Suddenly she said something in his ear and left brusquely, forcing him to join Chrome Black and the Joker. For a few minutes, Hermano tried to fathom why they were over there and he was here, sitting on a chair. He couldn't. Then he tried to decide whether he was satisfied or unsatisfied with the fact that he was sitting on the chair, far from the dance floor. He couldn't make up his mind. Maybe he wanted to get up and go over to the others. Maybe that was what he *should* do, even if he didn't want to. Maybe both things were false. Maybe he should have been at home. Maybe he should go home right now, change out of his jeans and into a pair of shorts, grab his Walkman and earphones, get his bike out of the garage and pedal through the night like a madman while listening to Motörhead full blast, until his legs grew weak and his calves cramped up. As he considered the possibility, he wasn't sure if it was what he really wanted to do, if it was just what he thought he should do, or if it was what he would have liked everyone else to know he had done. Or was it what he would have liked, some-how, *to be seen* doing? He thought that somewhere in this questioning, or in the actual act of a sense-less ride through the night, lay a decisive clue to his identity, the merging point of the person he was, the person he thought he was and the person everyone else saw.

In that film-like ambience, among so many inse-cure actors playing their roles, a single element stood out for its physical presence. Without his orange cap, Bonobo was dancing with Ingrid, their bodies close. His neck was at a straight angle to the parquet floor. His shaved head was held erect but tilted slightly downwards, his eyes apparently fixed on Ingrid's head, a good eight inches below his. Leading the dance, Bonobo's body barely seemed to move, while Ingrid's hips swayed softly. There was latent tension as the dance partners spun around, a play of domination, resistance and surrender. They were, in short, dancing properly. Whether he was aware of it or not, Bonobo knew what he was doing. He didn't usually take an interest in girls a lot younger than him. As he danced with little Ingrid, it was as if he were teaching her something.

Hermano glanced over his shoulder. Isabela's mother was watching him. She smiled affectionately when their eyes met. He gave her a little automatic smile in return and when he turned back to the dance floor he found Naiara's eyes staring into his, intrigued. It was disturbing, as if he'd suddenly found himself on a firing line. He looked at the ground, where there was no risk of any further eye contact with women. Another glass of Coke seemed a good pretext to get out of there. He stood, found himself a clean cup and an open bottle on a nearby table, and plodded towards the door, thinking he'd step outside for a breath of rain-laced air, maybe even convince himself to ditch the increasingly oppressive atmosphere of the party once and for all. Halfway there, the sight of a small disturbance in the scene he had been observing until a few moments earlier caused him to stop in his tracks. Isabela was holding Uruguay by the wrist, apparently trying to keep his arm away from some soft

part of her body. The gesture wasn't terribly overt,
but it was enough to suggest a situation of harass-
ment and resistance. Uruguay's other arm was
clasped forcefully to her back. His chin was hooked
over her neck like a clamp. She was saying something. Uruguay's eyes were still closed, and his lips
were contorted with the emission of some strange
noise that couldn't be heard over the music. They
were no longer turning, and held their positions as
if a brusque movement was being prepared by one
of the parties. Isabela raised her voice and now he
could make out what she was saying. She was telling Uruguay to let her go, saying the same thing
over and over, separated by identical pauses. One
by one, the people on the dance floor stopped to
see what was going on. Uruguay wouldn't let go
of Isabela, as if by insisting he still might, absurdly,
turn the situation in his favour again. She strug-
gled to get free more and more vigorously. It was
time to do something, and the realization brought
a tremor to Hermano because for a moment he
thought about intervening, separating them, some-
how immobilizing Uruguay and taking him
outside, but he did nothing of the sort and just
stood there, considering a whole catalogue of possible ways to approach Uruguay and fend off a
likely violent reaction, until Isabela gave Uruguay
a push and freed herself, except for her hand, which

he wouldn't let go of, and began to scream, and everyone but Hermano decided to intervene at the same time, including Isabela's mother, who ran to her daughter's aid and got an earful of what could only have been the lewdest of language coming from Uruguay's mouth. By now Hermano had convinced himself that the best thing to do was stay right where he was, drinking Coke. That was when Bonobo made his entrance, headbutting Uruguay in the teeth. Uruguay stumbled back about three steps and pushed off the wall to respond to the attack, planting a kangaroo kick in the middle of Bonobo's chest, leaving him breathless for a few seconds, at the mercy of a few more blows to the face. A clearing formed in the middle of the restaurant. The girls who hadn't raced outside screamed as they watched the fight. A few people tried to break it up and ended up taking a stray elbow or two. Bricky went as far as to pick up a chair and hurl it at them (the Recanto Espanhol had large, heavy wooden chairs with pointy corners), but it did no good. Uruguay weighed more and was stronger than Bonobo, but the outcome of the fight was predictable. The punches he received only stoked Bonobo's rage and he flew at Uruguay swinging his arms in a brutal sequence of blows, at a forward tilt, as if fighting his way through a furious flock of bats. A well-placed blow to

Uruguay's jaw left him groggy, allowing Bonobo to get him in a headlock and drag him in an ungentlemanly fashion into the street, where he made it very clear that that was no way to behave at a birthday party. Only then did some adult relatives emerge from their secret corners to bring the situation back under control. The music stopped, the lights came on, and the girls went to console Isabela.

Hermano watched the guests, including his own friends, leave in small groups on foot or in cars driven by the older ones. A taxi was called to take Uruguay, accompanied by Chrome Black, to the emergency room (there was a short debate about whether or not it was best to go first to a hospital or to an orthodontic clinic; no consensus was reached). Before leaving, Hermano needed to drain off the excess Coke in the men's room. When he opened the door, he found himself staring at Isabela's mother's backside, as she leaned over the toilet. Just then, she turned to Hermano.

'Ice, darling. Can you get me some ice from the kitchen?'

Only then did Hermano see Bonobo sitting on the toilet. The fleeting eye contact between the two of them was empty, no message was exchanged. Bonobo was pressing a white cloth to his mouth, but he took it away from time to time to call

Isabela's mother 'Aunty' and say things like 'Jeez, Aunty, it's not fair, Isabela's such a nice girl, this kind of thing really gets me mad', while 'Aunty' responded in nervous monosyllables as she doused balls of cotton wool in hydrogen peroxide.

Hermano went to the kitchen, found the freezer and an ice tray. The mission was almost insignificant, but it included him in what was going on and that was good. It was like visiting an actor's dressing room after a play. There was the star, sitting on the toilet, a weary and intimidating figure at the centre of attention. Isabela's mother took the ice cubes from Hermano, rolled them in the cloth and pressed it to Bonobo's lips, which were already swollen.

'Thanks,' said Bonobo, looking over her shoulder.

That slight, almost impersonal acknowledgement gave Hermano an enormous sense of satisfaction. He could hardly believe that until just a few hours earlier he'd been afraid of getting beaten up by Bonobo, and felt ashamed. A few minutes later, the two of them set out on foot for Esplanada, at first about two hundred yards apart, but heading the same way, and now they were walking side by side, each hearing the other's proximity.

After walking for a few blocks along the

shoulder of Serraria Road, they turned right on to Reservation Street. Here and there were parked cars and, under them, dogs and cats that had taken shelter from the rain there, sleeping or watching the night, their eyes points of light in the darkness. The street followed the crest of the hill and on the right was a long downward slope dominated by grey asbestos rooftops. They walked until they reached the top of the stairs where the downhill competitions took place. Bonobo stopped and sat on the first step. Hermano kept going, one step at a time, almost stopping as he looked over his shoulder, a word of goodbye stuck on his tongue. But it was Bonobo who spoke.

'Have a seat. Or are you going home now?'

Hermano came back and sat down.

'I'm gonna try and finish this before the sun comes up,' said Bonobo, holding up the still-full bottle of cachaça to analyse it.

'In't that a bit much?'

'Yep. But a guy's gotta try, right?'

'That whole thing with Uruguay was fucked up.'

'He was asking for it. What a dickhead, forcing himself on a girl like that, especially the birthday girl. You really not drinking?'

'I don't drink alcohol. I saw when he started groping her. I was just about to step in myself.'

'I've never liked that guy, although most

Uruguayans are pretty cool. Why don't you drink? Doctor's orders?'

'I could if I wanted to. Sorry 'bout that time on the field, it was an accident.'

Bonobo didn't reply. He just turned and looked Hermano in the eye for a second. The ensuing silence was long and Hermano thought bringing it up again had been a grave mistake, even though it had popped out of his mouth automatically, almost without thinking.

'See that plot of land down there?' said Bonobo, pointing with the bottle.

'Which one?'

'That one. Near the eucalyptus trees, down at the end. Almost at Police Hill. It's pretty small. There's a water tank next to it and a lamp post.'

'I see it.'

'It's my mum's. She said if I save up enough to build on it she'll give it to me.'

'You reckon you can?'

'I reckon so. I'm doing inspections for a car insurance company. In a year or two, maybe. If I work hard I'll get a promotion.'

The sound of crunching gravel began and grew in intensity until a yellow beam lit his back and a car sped up the street, invading the silence and then gradually vacating it. Hermano held out his hand, Bonobo read the gesture and, without any questions, offered him the bottle of cachaça. He took a small swig, which left a burning sensation on his lips. It was his first drink of alcohol and it would be his last, he was sure. He just felt an urgent need to have something new in his life. Now he was no longer someone who *never drank*, and was thus a different person. Switching personalities, or brusquely changing the course of his life, had always seemed unfeasible, nothing more than a source of anxiety and frustration, but in spur-of-the-moment gestures like that a whole world of possibilities opened up. Interfering with destiny suddenly seemed simple. Little by little, through small actions of the sort, maybe it was possible to gradually become someone else, someone not as quiet, who was able to incorporate into the plot of his own life the exquisite violence of comics, the virility and magnetism of his favourite movie heroes, the rugged ease of the actions and words of someone like . . . he had to own up to it now, not just to himself but to everyone – someone like Bonobo, a figure so ugly he was almost a caricature, whose greatest talent was beating up other people, but who embodied like no one else some kind of obscure ideal to which Hermano aspired. That swig of cachaça might be the first sign of a permanent bond, the first exchange among many that would grow into a meaningful friendship. In a few years' time, they might be good friends. If they joined forces, they might be able to save enough money to build a house on the land that Bonobo's mother had promised him. Hermano had only two years of high school left. He could get a part-time job during that time or, why not, simply drop out, open a bike repair shop, anything. He and Bonobo would share a place, their respective girlfriends would be almost permanent fixtures, they'd have the gang from Esplanada over for parties and to watch Grêmio matches on TV. Or not. Maybe the house idea wasn't so viable, just the delirium of a passing enthusiasm, but a variety of scenes of future possibilities flitted through Hermano's thoughts like the trailer for an action movie, a road movie, he and Bonobo driving down the continent along Argentinean highways, over the brown plains of Patagonia with snowy mountain ranges on the horizon, leaving a mark on the villages and in the memories of the people they met along the way, heading towards the deep south, to something immense and unspeakable, the climax of a journey. It was the vision of a life beyond the introspection of solitary exercise, an adventure for which he had been preparing himself for so many years, at last a concrete goal for all the unspecific expectation he had carried with him since some time in his childhood, an unfolding of the desire to take on and be taken on by the world. Hermano was exultant. Beside him, Bonobo looked absorbed in his own thoughts, and only the devil could have said what they were. They sat there without speaking for a long time, but it wasn't a problem, because to pass the time nothing seemed necessary but their mute presence, a telepathic tension between two interior monologues.

6.31 a.m.

When he was a child, Serraria Road ran through a semi-rural area that was progressively being taken over by lower-middle-class families. He had watched the gradual occupation of the southern-most part of Porto Alegre from birth through to his university years, witnessing the transformation of the landscape around him. He still had clear memories of when it was an almost virgin subdivision, each vacant lot holding its own secret – a living or dead animal, vestiges of a mysterious camp, a trail that appeared to lead somewhere previously unexplored and then petered out in the grass inexplicably. Returning now, years after moving into Adri's mother's apartment in Petrópolis and, more recently, into their three-bedroom house in Bela Vista, Esplanada's calling as a residential zone struck him with a profusion of apartment complexes, gated communities and a new supermarket. Cobbled streets and dirt roads had been tarmacked over. The hundreds of residences built over the last few years reminded him of the homes found on suburban housing estates, with two- or three-storey constructions on narrow properties, craning over one another for a view of the Guaíba. Most of these new houses looked like stacked crates with slight variations in size and lay-out, minuscule or non-existent front gardens, high metal fences topped with spikes and, in many cases, electric fences, double garages, colonial or French ceramic tiles, and white or horrible pastel-coloured walls. A giant display of cheap construction materials designed by an evil sect of civil engineers and lobotomized architects. He drove a few hundred yards down Serraria Road and turned on to Reservation Street. There, where most of the plots of land were occupied by older homes, the passing of time seemed to have brought fewer changes. The street had been tarmacked over, but the slimy granite pavements were there, the modest one-storey houses with gardens harmonized by the action of the years, and cement walls little more than three feet high, rusty steel dustbins, stray dogs rubbing muzzles with dogs behind bars or restrained by collars. They were banal but familiar things, like the repetitive birdsong that sounded like a bossa nova refrain. After four blocks and two turns, he found himself in front of the house he had lived in with his parents until he was twenty-five, now owned by a couple of young veterinarians who had three Siberian huskies, innumerable cats and a freshwater lobster. The dogs were in a fenced-off kennel to one side of the house, which now boasted a garden full of decorative plants and was protected by green steel bars. To his horror, he saw that the exposed brick walls of the formerly modest but cosy dwelling had been rendered and painted an awful salmon colour. The old guillotine windows with varnished wooden frames had been replaced with sliding windows with aluminium frames. But it all paled in comparison with the second storey, which had been added on more recently, covered with immaculate new tiles. It appeared to be an en suite with a balcony that had simply been fitted over the old roof without a thought for the overall harmony of the building. His parents, who now lived in an apartment in Auxiliadora bought with the money from the sale of the house, no doubt knew nothing of it. They'd be devastated if they did. His father not so much, as he had actually adapted well to the new suburb and, at the age of fifty-nine, continued to play tennis two or three times a week at União and to peruse – in reading glasses, face glued to the computer screen – several daily newspapers online, despite the macular degeneration that was progressively affecting the centre of his visual field and his ability to read. His mother was more attached to the old neighbourhood. She had left behind her friends and a provincial micro-universe which she had navigated effortlessly and comfortably, while the urban density of areas closer to the centre got on her nerves. Some two years earlier, he had insisted that his parents go through with the sale of the house and the move closer in, thinking of a not-so-distant future in which being close to their son, shops and medical clinics would be more important than the ramshackle bucolicism of the southern suburbs. He was no longer sure it had been such a good idea. The move was yet another example of his obstinate way of planning everything so far in advance, organizing life around him so that everything happened as planned in five, ten, twenty years' time. Only now did he see this clearly: his encouragement to sell the house in Esplanada had had more to do with his anticipation of his own future than his parents' interests. The realization, coupled with the sight of what the veterinarians had done to the house, made him feel like crap. Maybe it hadn't all been necessary. Not just the sale of the house and his parents' move, but everything. Everything he had done since that Sunday in 1991. The front door of the old family home, solid hardwood darkened with carnauba wax, was the only part of the house that appeared to have remained untouched, and now, staring at the door, he saw himself as a fifteen-year-old turning the oval doorknob and hearing the spring creak, still digesting the experience of his first visit to a cemetery, his first funeral, building a shelter amidst a mental storm, planning what his life would be like from then on as if he were planning his slow, obstinate transformation into a superhero who would re-emerge fifteen years later to be admired for his self-control and intelligence, for his stoicism and physical vigour, like the heavy front door that had remained oblivious to the world in transformation around it. Fifteen years earlier, he had decided to shut himself away, reading and studying, until he'd exhausted his ability to concentrate, going out only to tire his body with forty-mile bike rides to Lami or hour-long runs along the riverside promenade in Ipanema, as solitary a routine as possible, entirely focused on surpassing his own limits and demanding the utmost of himself, pushing himself to a level that few human beings could attain. He scouted around for the most difficult degree at the most demanding university in the state, and the trail led to the profession to which he felt he was clearly destined, the profession that would justify complete surrender to discipline and at the same time satisfy his fascination with blood and gore, an ambiguous feeling that involved an aesthetic attraction to violence and a frankly cowardly fear of the real thing. He would learn to tame his urges, to domesticate blood, to apply violence scientifically with the noble aim of curing other human beings. He mapped out the rest of his life in the week following the funeral. He would become a doctor. The best. In the second semester, he finished his second year of high school with marks higher than 9.2, and the following year he didn't have a single mark under 9. Four months before graduating, he started an after-hours prep course for the university entrance exams and began to read newspapers and Brazilian literary classics well into the night, in addition to carefully rereading biology, chemistry, maths, history, literature, physics and English textbooks, doing exercises and copying out long passages by hand until the friction of the pencil made a painful yellow callus on the side of his right middle finger. He stopped watching films, reading comics and going out. He pulled away almost completely from his friends in Esplanada, who still came looking for him with accusations of 'Hey, stranger' and 'Where you been?' but after a few weeks they gave up. He resisted his parents' attempts to get him to see a psychologist. He wasn't traumatized. He wasn't trying to get over a difficult experience. He didn't feel alienated. He was just looking for an objective. And in so doing he came first in the entrance exam to study medicine at the Federal University of Rio

Grande do Sul. The prep course asked if they could use his photograph for a publicity campaign, but he turned down the request. He humbly received congratulations from friends and family and ignored his fame, which was spreading through the neighbourhood. It was just the beginning. With the same energy, he plunged into six years of med school, a two-year residency in general surgery and another two years of plastic surgery at Ernesto Dornelles Hospital, until he opened his own practice at the age of twenty-eight. With his age, skill and appearance, he quickly became a well-kept secret among a small but devout group of clients who came to him to correct physical flaws or, in most cases, to fix bodies that only needed fixing if held to beauty standards as unrealistic as they were omnipresent. The more he tried to convince a female client that this or that implant or treatment was unnecessary, the more adamant she would become, and in extreme cases he had no choice but to refuse to proceed. Men were more easily persuaded to try diets, exercise, or simply do something to give their self-esteem a tweak. At any rate, his reputation as a young prodigy with a tendency to challenge his patients' wishes, but who in the operating theatre was an incomparable sculptor, had been growing for about a year now. His hands were large and firm. In them, a scalpel became a tiny, delicate instrument. He explained with great patience and in detail the risks of each operation. None of his breast-augmentation patients went on to the operating table without first understanding what capsular retraction was and the chances of it happening, which would require surgical correction or even removal of the implant; nor did they go under the knife without fully understanding that prostheses weren't for ever and would have to be replaced due to the useful life of the silicone implant or the normal thinning of the skin tissue and consequent sagging of the breasts, which would require future surgeries, etc., etc. For the vast majority of his patients, however, the violence of surgical intervention and the post-op suffering were almost insignificant aspects of a blessed procedure that solved a whole range of insecurities and problems once and for all. Beauty magazines led people to believe that mammoplasty, chemical peels and liposculpture were ways to change one's appearance that were as quick and inoffensive as a haircut. He'd never forgotten how the mother of one of his first young patients had broken down and wept when he told her it was possible to perform breast-augmentation surgery on her daughter, for which she had saved a generous portion of her wages as a department-store sales assistant for almost two years. It was as if they'd found a kidney donor after years of anxious waiting. Her eighteen-year-old daughter's chest puffed out with emotion, pushing forward the small but shapely breasts that would soon be enlarged by the transaxillary placement of prostheses beneath the pectoralis major muscle, and her eyes sparkled and darted randomly about the office, probably imagining scenes from a near future filled with predatory looks from men, her friends' envy, self-confidence at parties and exhibitionism at the beach. That was when he understood that his patients needed what he had to offer with an intensity that obscured the risks and justified any cost, discomfort or bleeding. He did his part: he spelled out the pros, cons and consequences fully and sincerely. Then he did his job with tremendous attention to detail. His biggest secret was that, deep down, he was unconvinced by the aesthetic result of most of the procedures he performed. Rhinoplasties and otoplasties to correct deformities or shapes too distant from the anatomical standard were one thing, but he didn't like the artificiality of a breast replaced with a prosthesis and he knew that abdominal liposuction was, in most cases, like papering over cracks. He thought that both men and women, striving to measure up to dubious beauty standards, went overboard with the interventions they sought. But it was his job. He had spent nearly half his life obtaining the necessary knowledge and experience to be what he was: a specialist in aesthetic medicine. It was a career he was proud of. It had demanded great sacrifice and effort on his part, and the only unexpected disruption had been Adri, the girl with wavy waist-length hair, bright teeth and eyes, and ornamental gestures like those of a dancer from the Orient, whose waxy skin smelled of warm stone and, after hours of sex, left a unique, indescribable taste in his mouth that coated his tongue and teeth like the fat from certain meats. Adri, the girl who had made him rethink his conviction that even the company of a woman was an obstacle to his heroic quest. What would have become of him if he really had stayed single for the last fifteen years? Feeling a little guilty, he wondered if he hadn't demanded too much of his wife the last few years, as if she'd had to prove on a daily basis that she deserved her role within the life of her husband, the man who'd once told her he'd do everything in his power to make her happy. Repressing the urge to self-critique, he turned the key in the ignition and cruised in first gear through the streets of Esplanada, where human life was beginning to announce its presence in the form of a uniformed doorman cycling up a hill in first gear or a woman in tracksuit bottoms swinging her arms and hips on her morning walk. He wondered if Adri had got up early, right after he'd left. It was likely, seeing as how she probably hadn't been asleep. He retrieved his mobile from the passenger seat and switched it on. There was voicemail. He pressed some buttons and listened to the phone operator's message, expecting to hear Adri immediately afterwards, but the voice he heard was Renan's. 'Whatsup dude? It's six-forty and it ain't like you to be late. Did you chicken out? Ha ha. Alarm didn't go off? If you get this, call me. I'm just hanging, waiting for you. Bonete might run away. Big kiss on your soul, bro.' 'Go fuck yourself,' he grumbled, as he punched in his home number. Adri picked up on the third ring. 'Adri?' 'Is that you? Where are you?' 'Did I wake you up?' 'Renan called here, asking where you were. I told him you'd left more than half an hour ago.' 'If he calls again, tell him I went to Bolivia by myself.' 'Where are you? Is everything OK?' 'Can I tell you a secret?' 'Huh?' 'I want to tell you something I've never told anyone before.' 'Is everything OK? Renan –' 'Did you know you're the only woman I've ever had sex with?' 'What the fuck?' 'I'm ser-ious. You were my first.' 'Come off it . . . you were twenty-three when I met you.' 'Twenty-four. Any-way, I just wanted to tell you.' 'Why now? Where are you?' 'Bye. When Nara wakes up, tell her I called to say I love her so much.' 'Where are you? You're scaring me now. Are you going to get

Renan?' 'No.' 'Oh, God.' 'Don't worry. Bye.'
'Wait.' 'Bye.' He hung up, put the phone in silent
mode and tossed it back into the passenger seat.
The screen lit up to indicate an incoming call but
he ignored it. He was passing Esplanada's old
square. It was all there still: the football pitch, the
'royal box', where the girls used to sit and watch
the boys play, the merry-go-round, the monkey
bars and playground equipment, except that now,
besides being corroded, faded and worn, it all
looked like a miniature model of the square he
remembered. It was as if objects and places had
shrunk with the years, just as the years themselves
had grown shorter. He reached the first intersection
and didn't know which way to turn. Truth be told,
he didn't have the faintest idea why he was there.
All he knew was that he wasn't going home just
now, much less to pick up Renan, go to Bolivia or
even to leave the city on his own, less again to
return to the clinic the following Monday. His
mobile screen continued to flash. He flipped a coin
in his mind and decided to turn left and drive
around the back of the square, where there used to
be an area of forest that now looked like a dozen
trees and a small adjacent area covered with pointy
molasses grass, which resembled light-green hair
with violet tips. 'The lost era,' he thought, the line
from Elomar's song still echoing in his mind,

although the third track of the CD was now playing. The car was doing less than ten miles an hour,
the engine almost cutting out. On his right, the
morning sun struck the lamp posts and cast shadows
across the street diagonally. He had the weird
impression that the posts marked graves positioned
at regular intervals along the pavement, like the
eccentric tombstones of an unknown civilization.
The sound of footsteps and a shout or grunt caught
his attention and made him glance to his left again.
A boy of fifteen or sixteen was sprinting across the
flattest part of the square. Another eight to ten
appeared behind him. He stopped the car and
watched to see where the fugitive and his pursuers
were headed. There wouldn't be any police around,
especially at that hour. The boy being chased ran
full pelt, jumped over an obstacle and disappeared
momentarily behind some trees, to reappear immediately afterwards, further away. The others would
eventually catch up and he'd be beaten until he
passed out. That was life. What could you do? The
group crossed an intersection and disappeared
around a corner. It was time to move on, but where
to? Maybe Lami. Spend Sunday there, have a beer,
see what had changed – people said the water really
was clean now. Then he could decide what was to
be of his life. He put the car into first, drove fifty feet
and stopped again. He pulled up the handbrake.

He knew what he had to do. He climbed into the back seat, which had been laid down to become an extension of the car boot, released a few straps on his backpack and pulled out the brand-new ice axe that he'd bought especially for the expedition. It was shaped like a small pickaxe and incredibly light for its size. He held it by its handle, which was about one and a half feet long, and briefly gazed at the sharp stainless-steel blade, which looked like a heron's beak. Then he climbed back into the driver's seat, released the handbrake, put the car into reverse and floored it.

NAIARA

Hermano pushed his bike up the cement path that ran across the lawn, knocked on Bonobo's door and, sitting on his bike frame while he waited, admired the album cover of Led Zeppelin's *Houses of the Holy* for the fiftieth time, trying to find a new interpretation or detail he hadn't noticed before in the montage of naked children climbing a large pile of rocks in Ireland.

Naiara opened the door with a smile, said hi, and continued vigorously stirring a sticky mixture of condensed milk and chocolate powder in a tempered glass mug.

He asked if Bonobo was home.

She said he wasn't.

He asked if she knew when he'd be back.

She said she didn't, but if he'd only come to leave a record for Bonobo, she could give it to him later.

Hermano didn't just want to lend him the record; in one of his first conversations with Bonobo after walking home together the night of Isabela's party, they had discovered they were both Led Zeppelin fans, and now he was hoping for an opportunity to spend some time with his new friend. Lending him the album was merely a pretext, so he decided to leave a message saying he'd come back later.

Instead of saying goodbye and closing the door, Naiara almost choked as she tried to swallow a spoonful of the condensed-milk mixture too quickly. She had suddenly remembered that her brother had said he'd be back before lunch, which meant he shouldn't be more than ten or fifteen minutes, she was positive, so Hermano could come in and wait.

From the notable absence of any cooking smells, domestic noise or sign of movement inside the house, Hermano gathered that no lunch was being prepared and that Naiara, in baggy tracksuit bottoms with oval-shaped leather knee patches and a red boob tube that her tiny breasts didn't look capable of holding up for long, was home alone, tricking her stomach with spoonfuls of an improvised, calorie-packed sludge.

She opened the door a little wider for Hermano to come in, and asked if he wanted anything to eat or drink.

He said no.

The living-room floor and furniture were made of *ipê* wood, whose caramel-streaked, dark-brown grain gave the place a slightly sinister, cavernous feel. There was a strong smell of wood and clay, hemp rugs on the floor and embroidered woollen hangings on the brick walls. Even on a hot day, with most of the windows open, the interior of the house was chilly and poorly lit.

Naiara told Hermano to have a seat on the sofa, but he took the armchair and she ended up sitting on the sofa herself.

He leaned over, gripped the tip of his shoe and began to stretch his calf muscle.

Naiara asked what record it was.

He gave her a succinct description of the album and his reasons for liking it.

She left her mug on the sofa, stood, and came to peer over his shoulder at the cover of the album on his lap.

He told her his theory that the children climbing the pile of rocks were Robert Plant's.

With her hand on the back of the chair, Naiara sat on the arm and leaned forward to stare at the album, very close to Hermano.

He inhaled the choc-milky breath that she breathed on his ear at regular intervals, while one of her little breasts pressed against his shoulder, which made him think of chocolate-filled pastry pillows, his favourite dessert.

She leaned her cheek against Hermano's face.

The album slid off his lap on to the floor.

She began softly rubbing her cheek on his face, up and down.

He sat there stiffly, straight-backed, looking at her out of the corner of his eye, his face unmoving, as if it were just a manly support for a fragile and needy girl to rub her cheek on.

She went on rubbing.

Hermano's impassivity slowly crumbled as he felt growing tremors in his hands and legs, and he began to give in, his control of the situation slipping away, until he had no choice but to turn his head a little and allow his lips to meet Naiara's in an indecisive kiss, trying his hardest to disguise the fact that it was his first.

Whispering in his ear, Naiara suggested they go to her room.

Everything in it that could be red was red. Red pillowcases, red blanket, burgundy curtains. The wall behind the bed was dark red. In a corner, atop a trunk, was an abandoned doll cemetery, with everything from life-sized babies to voluptuous little women in miniature. Some, without any clothing, sported exaggerated deformations of the human anatomy, with curves and details in pink plastic, their faces crudely made up with red lipstick and other kinds of ink and beauty products. On the ceiling, constellations of glow-in-the-dark stickers were opaque green blobs in the daylight.

A jumble of clothing and plush toys occupied the bed, shelves, and spaces in the wardrobe. Underwear, tops, sandals, bears, badgers, dolphins. A small red glass-topped dressing table with a mirror was covered with a thorny flora of bobby pins, butterfly clips, perfume bottles, nail polish, brushes, combs, pencils and a can of hairspray.

'I can't believe you're here,' said Naiara.

Hermano sat on the bed and ran his fingers over her slender waist, stroked her soft little belly, a flat surface with a shallow belly button that looked more like a scar. He held her by the hips. Her tiny pelvis was a bone to which other articulated pieces were attached. Oddly, he couldn't stop thinking about the internal structure of her body, its parts, and how they all fitted together and moved, irrigated with lubricating fluids, the warmth and silkiness of their coverings. One half of his mind processed this data and replied 'machine', 'doll', 'child'. The other half insisted on 'woman', and he sensed that his arousal depended on the insistence of the second half.

Naiara ran her fingers through Hermano's oily light-brown hair and she straddled him on the bed, digging her knees into the mattress like the stabilizers of a backhoe loader. Beneath her, Hermano was almost horizontal, leaning back on his outstretched arms.

'Woman,' Hermano repeated mentally to himself. With the second, third and each consecutive kiss he felt a little more secure; with each one he learned a little lesson. He wasn't really sure what he was allowed to touch, but he gradually realized it was everything. She let him. He wanted to pull down her boob tube, but no, he didn't dare do that.

As she pulled off his shirt, she asked if he knew that all the girls had the hots for him, that his body was their main topic of conversation and that they all dreamed of getting him into bed before anyone else, because none of them had ever had sex with him or even kissed him, and it was really unfair of him to share his body only with the girls from his school or wherever the girls he hooked up with were, neglecting his neighbourhood admirers. What a lack of community spirit. Snobbery, cruelty.

Hermano brusquely jerked down her boob tube with both hands. Her petite breasts were capable of triggering the action-reaction he wanted, making him stop thinking, stop seeing inside and through the body of that little creature ('woman'), that girl ('woman', *woman* . . .), so he trained his attention on them. But fear was beginning to set in and he was reluctant to carry on. Couldn't they just leave it at that? Couldn't that just be it?

But Naiara wanted to go further, and quickly.

In no time, she had removed all their clothes. She sniffed his chest like a dog fixated on a scent in the grass, squeezed his arm muscles.

Then, suddenly, it was all over for Hermano. Self-consciousness got the better of him. There was something ridiculous about that skinny girl rubbing herself against him with demented eyes. She was a child acting like a woman. It was Naiara, *Bonobo's little sister.* He began to see everything from the outside, like a camera installed in the ceiling. The goddamn camera was his only lover. Like a betrayed wife who, acting on intuition, calls her husband at work just as he is taking his secretary from behind on the desk in his office, the imaginary camera that accompanied Hermano everywhere also had an infallible sixth sense and loathed to be usurped. Sometimes the camera would appear at a crucial moment in his existence; other times it recorded the reality of banal, solitary moments, like when he was running in Ipanema and it started to rain, when he got off the bus and walked through the front gate of his school, as he rode his bike at high speed for hours on end, crossing several neighbourhoods, or when he climbed Police Hill as if he were alone, practically ignoring the company of his friends, because it was just him, the hill and the *camera*. It wasn't merely the feeling of being watched, imagining anonymous witnesses of scenes in his life. It was as if he had left his own body to become the observer. He was the one operating the camera, the one who left the scene, crossed the membrane between reality and the imagination and chose a seat in the darkness of the empty movie theatre. Why would things be any different now? Hermano was no longer there. Naiara was interacting with an automaton, and both were being observed by his true consciousness, hovering like a cynical spectre over the red jumble of the bedroom, looking for the best angles and light to show the protagonist's sad and solitary feats to best effect. And what the camera saw now was a thirteen-year-old girl doing everything in her power, using her entire precocious repertoire of techniques, to try to blow life into a dummy.

Hermano took hold of Naiara's head, looked at her perplexed face and said:

'Come here.'

He was lying crosswise on the bed with the back of his head propped against the wall. He gently tugged on her head and, obeying his command, she crawled up the bed and straddled him again. He ran his thumbs over her lips, revealing sharp little teeth, the bottom ones still new-looking and serrated.

'What do you want me to do?' she asked.

'Bite me.'

Completely serious, like a nurse listening carefully to a surgeon's orders, she asked where.

'Anywhere. Here,' he said, indicating his chest with his chin.

She bit him one, two, three, four times in different places, holding each bite for a few seconds with enough force to leave deep grooves that stung.

'Want me to bite you harder?'

'Bite me as hard as you've ever wanted to bite someone in your life.'

'That might be preeetty hard.'

'Let's see.'

Naiara took a chunk of muscle between her teeth and began to clench them. He took a deep breath and held it. The pain grew proportionate to the pressure, and he was surprised she had the courage to bite him like that, harder and harder, without letting go, until the nerves in his body felt like they were on fire. The moment arrived when his defence mechanisms demanded that he do something, but he resisted. As he inhaled and held his breath, the agony he felt was almost unbearable, but each exhalation brought a shudder of pleasure that was intensified by the thought that her teeth were probably piercing his skin, sinking into his flesh, all the way to the gums. The mental image of gums and the sound of the word 'flesh' excited him. The gums, teeth and tongue in that tiny mouth, fastened to his chest. To stop the saliva running from her mouth, she sucked in air without releasing the bite, making a slurpy noise like a small animal's hiss of warning. As it reached his ears, that singular sound brought on a climax of sorts.

When Naiara finally released her jaw and pulled her face back, he saw his blood on her pointy little teeth, and she saw the oval wound she had made above and to the left of his right nipple. It was superficial, but visually impressive. He stood up, chin pressed to his neck, watching the blood well up, bead, and slide unhurriedly down his chest. Then he turned to the mirror on the dressing table and stood there, frozen, contemplating what he saw until Naiara appeared behind him with a folded tissue and pressed it to the wound, stroking his stomach with the other hand. For the first time, he found her pretty. Her thick lips and nose that reminded him of an electrical socket were an exotic complement to her somewhat sinister black eyes and long eyelashes. Her face was very thin, but there was still some volume to her cheeks. A red droplet had almost reached his navel. Her hand smeared it across his skin. Hermano mentally recorded the entire scene. He knew he'd never forget it.

A few minutes later, Naiara put on her underwear and boob tube, left the room and came back a minute later with an enormous plastic cup of Coke.

Hermano was still undressed. It seemed appropriate to remain like that, lying on the bed, as if nothing out of the ordinary were going on. Naiara sat down beside him, ran a finger around the bite mark and asked if it hurt much. He nodded. A whole array of scars from various scratches and cuts was exposed in its totality to another person for the first time. The marks caught Naiara's eye. On his left shin was a recent injury, a vertical cut almost five inches long, the result of his foot slipping off the pedal of his bike two days earlier. It was a little inflamed, the skin around it somewhat red.

'You're always taking a tumble, man. You'd think it was on purpose.'

'I ride a lot. And I go fast. Sometimes I fall. I reckon that's it.'

As she continued to explore his body, running her finger over every scar she found, Hermano made up his mind that as soon as he left there he'd head home, put on his running shoes and go for a run, and he'd probably run until he dropped. For the first time, he felt able to share a small detail of his gallery of habits (that is, 'perversions') which he considered abnormal (that is, 'shameful') and which were a source of ongoing perplexity and embarrassment for him because he wasn't very sure why he insisted on doing such things. All he knew was that he needed to do them, and behind them was the insinuation of a mystery, which attracted him.

'This scar here near the elbow . . . is from when I fell while I was running.'

'That's an ugly one.'

'It was on purpose. I do that sometimes. I go for a run, and I run normally for half an hour, and then I go as fast as I can. Full on. I usually start down in Ipanema and head up the quieter streets towards Esplanada, taking the hardest routes, where the roads aren't paved, through vacant land, sandy patches, the forest, or even down the middle of the street. I go full throttle, eyes practically closed, slipping when I go around corners and jump over things, until I eventually trip myself up, step in a hole, or stumble and fall. I don't stop until I've messed myself up. When I'm running I'm shit-scared, because I know what's going to happen sooner or later, and it's never something small – I really do hurt myself. That's how I got this one on my arm here. I lost a chunk of flesh. It was a bloody scab for about ten days. I also cut myself here under the chin, see? Another time I fell hands-first and had to go to hospital to get the stones removed. Look at this here. And here. And it's more or less the same with my bike. When I fall. It isn't always an accident, if you know what I mean. Last year I broke a rib. At least I think I did, because I could *feel* it was broken. It kind of cracked and I felt shooting pains, like the tip of a knife digging in here. But I didn't tell anyone. I hid it from my parents. The pain began to ease up and after a few weeks it stopped. I don't know why I do it.'

Silence. As if Naiara had asked him a question, Hermano repeated:

'I don't know why.'

'I've got a crush on you, you know?'

Hermano laughed.

'We don't even know each other.'

'Oh, I know you.'

'How can you know someone if you only see them around the place?' He took the cup of Coke from her and had a sip. The subject made him ill at ease. He'd have preferred to be talking about himself, defending himself, rather than hearing that she had a thing for him.

'You know when I first saw you? We'd only just moved here. About two years ago. I still didn't know anyone and I'd go out alone, hoping to meet people. It was my second or third day here. I went for a walk and ended up sitting at the top of the stairs, checking out the view. It was all new to me. It was a Sunday. It was cool to sit and see smoke from barbecues drifting up everywhere you looked, all the way over to Ipanema, Vila dos Remédios and Ponta Grossa, in the distance, the smell of coal and meat in the air. Then you appeared and started climbing the stairs. You were going quickly, two steps at a time. And that turns me on, seeing a guy climb stairs two at a time. Almost running, but not running, taking long strides. You can feel the effort of each leg, you know?'

'Ah, come on.'

'I'm serious. But listen. When you got halfway up, I realized you weren't coming up two steps at a time – it was *three at a time*. I'd never seen anyone do that before. And you were doing it so confidently, so effortlessly, that at the time it looked like it was two at a time. It stuck in my mind. It was like the stairs had been made to be climbed three at a time. It was so elegant. When you were near me, you nodded and looked away quickly. You were really serious. Dripping with sweat.'

'I must have been coming back from a run.'

'You can't imagine the state you left me in. I wanted to follow you to see where you lived, but my legs were too weak.'

'How old were you at the time?'

'Twelve. Or eleven. No, I'd already turned twelve.'

'You were a bit of an early starter, no?'

'Jeez, men can be stupid.'

'But aren't you? At the age of twelve you . . .'

'Wanna know how old I was when I came for the first time?'

'How old?'

'Four. I used to get turned on watching Spectreman.'

'No way.'

'I didn't really know what was going on, of course, but I remember it well and now I know it was sexual. I use to love watching *Spectreman*. I found him fascinating. Something about his face. It was hard and serious, made of metal, I think. Those fights with monsters. He'd be taking a beating and then he'd shoot a beam at them and win, but his face was always the same. It turned me on. How could he be so expressionless? I wasn't sure if it was really his face or if there was another face behind the mask. At any rate, I was hypnotized, and I'd feel this thing, this agitation. If his face didn't move, he probably didn't have any emotions, but I always knew when Spectreman was sad, or angry, or in pain. It was as if only I knew. I had a special connection with him.'

'I'd never thought of Spectreman as sexually potent, but if you say so . . .'

'Potent, that's the word! But it was his face. And then one day I watched the episode where the Monster Salamander breathes fire right in his face, and he goes blind. His eyes sort of melt and there are those two balls of deformed iron in the middle of his face. And he can't fight any more. I remember he suffered for ages, he couldn't see, he was completely disoriented. And that was the bit that drove me crazy. Because blind men turn me on too.'

'Get out of here.'

'Yep, even now. I've forgotten about Spectreman, but blind men . . . ooh. I just got goose pimples. As I watched the episode I started touching myself down there. Like, *there*. I always did when Spectreman came on. But when he went blind it was amazing. And then I had that feeling for the first time, but I only understood what it was a long time later. But I remember it perfectly.'

'What else turns you on besides Spectreman, blind men, and men climbing stairs two steps at a time?'

'Let's see . . . vampires. Vampires biting women's necks. When they sink their teeth in and then take them out, and their mouths are covered in blood, and there are those two little holes in the woman's neck. Oh, yeah. Vampires.'

'Right, so that's your fantasy. Blind vampires with metal faces that climb stairs three steps at a time. Super normal. And I thought *I* was the sick one.'

Naiara laughed.

'Yep, and that's exactly what you are. A blind vampire with a metal face that climbs stairs three steps at a time. Now you'd better get dressed, 'cause my mum and brother are in the living room and when I went to get Coke they asked me who the album on the floor belonged to.'

6.43 A.M.

He drove around the corner in reverse, stopped, put the car into first and accelerated after the boys. He immediately recognized the street, although the vacant land had given way to new residences. The thick forest on his right remained untouched, an island of green on to which the houses still hadn't dared encroach. As a child, he had often explored the narrow trails that ran through the forest, jumping over streams, looking for the giant Goliath birdeater spiders that clambered over tree trunks like enormous hairy hands. He saw the youths running down the middle of the street two hundred yards in front of him. As he sped towards them, he glanced to his right, looking for the old paint can hanging from a branch, but couldn't see it. It had been a long time: someone must have taken it down. He was certain the path to the clearing was nearby. That meant he'd already passed the lamp post. He could see two of them reflected in the rear-view mirror. Which one was it? He drove on, gripping the steering wheel and ice axe with the same broad hand. The engine roared as it strained in second at almost forty-five miles an hour. A hundred yards ahead, he saw one of the pursuers catch up with the fugitive, grab him by the T-shirt and bring him down. They hit the ground violently and rolled across the dirty tarmac, throwing up a cloud of dust. The boy who had been fleeing looked like he wanted to get up. He leaned on one arm and tried to sit, but it was as if he'd offered his head to the next pursuer, who took the penalty kick. The impact made his head fly back at a horrific angle, dragging the rest of his body behind it. Fifty yards. Now all of the eight or nine boys had arrived and were kicking and punching him as he lay on the ground, trying in vain to move, waiting for a chance to make a run for it. Thirty yards. The handle of the ice axe slipped in his sweaty palm. He saw the entire scene from above, as if the car were accompanied by a crane camera, speeding towards the fight. His numerical disadvantage was huge, but this time he wasn't going to hide. Twenty yards. He remembered the nitro-fuelled V8 in *Mad Max 2*, tearing through the desert wasteland with a gang of bloodthirsty outlaws right behind it. He had to face them this time. Ten yards. He wasn't just imagining scenes from the movie. Now he *was* Mad Max: he had embodied the road warrior. He wanted to throw the Montero into a slide but didn't know how. He jammed on the brake and the car skidded towards the thugs, whose reflex was to scatter, although they still hadn't fully grasped what was going on. He opened the car door and jumped out, holding the ice axe. The boy was still on the ground, moving without going anywhere, his face smeared with blood. The gang turned to face him. Mad Max returned their defiant looks, brandished the axe and took a step towards the injured boy. The gang members were also youths of about sixteen. Only one, with a beard, looked a little older. They were boys, at the pinnacle of their illusion of invincibility, hungry for opportunities to test their physical vigour and avenge themselves of the cosmic injustice of having been born, muscles ripped after afternoons of pumping iron at the gym, nearing their sexual peak. At thirty, he was the only tired veteran there. The gang cursed him. He hesitated, not sure if he should attack or wait. Attack which one? A hero couldn't hesitate. The boy received another kick in the head. The bearded one came towards him with a piece of wood. Mad Max was paralysed. The blow was aimed at his head. He dodged it and the wood grazed his ear, which began to burn. With a precise blow he buried the tip of the ice axe into the thigh of the enemy, who howled and staggered backwards. Another three came at him. The boy on the ground realized he was no longer the centre of attention and scrambled up. He raised the ice axe into the air, like a savage showing off his weapon in a war dance. It was his sawn-off shotgun. He noted something solid flying towards him a split second before a piece of ceramic tile struck him in the middle of the forehead. He couldn't see for about five seconds and felt blood oozing over the corner of his eye. He took a punch. He took several. He gave up trying to use the ice axe with precision, as he would to climb a frozen waterfall, and began swinging wildly at the air, eyes half closed, hitting God knows what, but definitely hitting things. One of his opponents backed away howling, hands clasped to his face. The others let up for a moment. That was good. They were reassessing the danger of the serrated tip of that miniature axe. The victim was standing now and punched one of his aggressors in the Adam's apple, making him drop to the ground, inert. Someone smashed a window of the Montero with a rock. The car. He remembered the car. He shouted to the boy to get in. Three or four gang members had now retreated to a cautious distance, while another three or four approached the car, ready to attack. Overcome with fury now, instead of protecting himself or backing off, he flew at them with the axe raised. Out of the corner of his eye, he saw the boy climbing into the car. He was kicked in the kidney and in quick succession sank the axe into the shoulder of the son of a bitch who had kicked him. 'The guy's crazy!' someone shouted. He roared, calling them all to fight. The pain shooting through his head dazed him. He could taste blood. It wasn't the first time, but this time it was the blood of bravery, not cowardice. It tasted different, better. He swallowed it greedily, licked his lips. They pelted him with stones. One hit his collarbone like a punch. He took a few more steps forward, defying the gang. They were leaving. Walking and throwing stones rather than running, but leaving. The one who'd been punched in the Adam's apple was carried by his companions. The bearded one was limping. Another was still pressing his hands to his face and staggered along, almost running, howling, helped by two pals. He glanced at the car. The boy had climbed in and was crouched on the floor on the passenger side, petrified, peering over the dashboard. Without taking his eyes off the aggressors, he returned to the Montero walking backwards. He touched its hot black hood and noticed the shards of broken windscreen scattered across it. He saw a few locals watching the tumult from doorways and windows, with puffy eyes and faces still creased from sleep. He climbed into the car, tossed the axe behind the driver's seat, started the engine, drove back to Serraria Road and put his foot down. The boy in the

passenger seat peeled off his white T-shirt that said
GAUCHOS DO EVERYTHING BETTER and used it to
clean his face, but when he pulled it away and looked
at it, blood streamed again from his nostrils and a
large cut in his eyebrow. He didn't seem to notice
and leaned back in the seat, holding the blood-
stained shirt in his lap, breathing heavily with his
eyes half-closed. 'Hold it to your face.' The boy
looked at him. 'Tilt your head back a bit, like this.
Press it on your nose and here on your eyebrow.'
The boy did as he was told. His face was swelling
up. 'You're bleeding from cuts on your knees and
elbows too. I'm taking you to a hospital, hang in
there.' He drove down Serraria Road at seventy-five
miles an hour and took a left on Juca Batista at the
new roundabout. The avenue he had driven down
just a few minutes earlier was now much busier. He
wove his way around a bus and half a dozen cars,
changing lanes brusquely. The boy was going to
need a few stitches, as well as X-rays, and everything indicated that his nose, which wouldn't stop
bleeding, was fractured. He decided to take him to
the emergency room at Mãe de Deus. Only then
did he remember to look at his own face in the rear-
view mirror. The worst thing was the wound at the
top of his forehead, where the piece of tile had hit
him. It was small but deep. Blood streamed from it
down both sides of his face and around the bridge

of his nose. Bad blood, black. The type that was good to get out of your system, to make room for clean new blood, the kind that ran through the veins deep inside. The boy was silent, staring through the closed window at the landscape. He was stunned and hunched over with pain, but at the same time showed a calm and resistance that you wouldn't expect from someone his age. He didn't look drunk. Of all the youths he had tended to during his residency, few had been able to stay so cool in a situation like that unless they were numbed by alcohol. It probably wasn't the first time he'd taken a beating. 'What happened?' 'What?' said the boy. A few seconds later, without any further prompting, he said, 'The one with the beard wanted to beat me up. The others helped.' 'Why did he want to beat you up?' 'Dunno.' The boy must have known, but it didn't matter. He was retracing the route he'd travelled that morning, but at three times the speed. The air was slowly acquiring the viscous texture of muggy days, and the temperature seemed to creep higher with each passing minute. 'He was gawking at me the whole party, so I stared back. When I left he came after me,' added the boy, who held the bloodied T-shirt away from his nose and mouth in order to speak. His skin was tanned; his curls looked as if they'd grown unchecked for months after having been shorn off, forming an irregular bloom that was comically bushy at the sides. A scar on the right side of his abdomen indicated he'd had an appendix removed some six months earlier. 'I don't have health insurance,' he mumbled. 'No sweat, I'm a doctor.' Never in his life had those words sounded so artificial coming out of his mouth. *I'm a doctor.* He was a doctor, of course. He remembered each stage of his interminable medical training and specialization, but it was as if each day of that effort had been recorded with a chalk mark on a cell wall. He was a doctor, but from the moment he'd awoken that morning he hadn't felt like one any more. He changed gears aggressively, the tyres squealing as he turned corners. It had been a long time since he'd surrendered so readily to fantasy. He remembered how in his youth he'd roamed the unknown streets of Esplanada on his Caloi Cross with balloon tyres, imagining himself a unique breed of adventure sportsman, blazing trails through vacant plots of land and over pavements packed with obstacles, in search of the city block that no other cyclist had ever successfully completed, so immersed in his heroic distortion of reality that he often experienced reality itself as a pause within an existence in which fantasy was the norm. The truth was: he was an up-and-coming plastic surgeon who had unjustifiably aborted a mountain-climbing expedition he'd been planning for months with his best friend, walked out on an atmosphere of marital acrimony that could have been resolved quickly with a little compassion and a few well-chosen words, and, in a kind of knee-jerk reaction, had taken a detour to the neighbourhood where he'd been born and raised, where he'd been surprised by an act of violence and had ended up intervening in a way he'd never imagined himself capable, and now he was doing the right thing, taking the injured boy and himself to an emergency room. But ever since he'd driven past the turn-off to Renan's house, he'd been gripped by the idea that he was in fact a solitary renegade deserting all ties to his life to seek something in his origins, driving his vehicle through a hostile land until chance provided him with the opportunity to do justice with bravery. He'd saved the boy's life, and now he was going to the place where they'd wait until their wounds healed. It was the moment in films, comic books and adventure novels when a man discovered his true nature and became a hero. He was so caught up in the fantasy that the phrase 'I'm a doctor' had sounded artificial, totally alien to who he really was and everything that was happening that Sunday morning. 'Someone's calling you,' said the boy, holding out his mobile, which was flashing in silent mode. The caller ID indicated that it was from Renan's home number. He answered. 'Hi, Renan.' 'Hey, man, what's going on?' 'Have a nice sleep, Renan?' 'Where are you? I've been ringing you non-stop since six-thirty.' 'I stopped the car and took on the lot of them, Renan. I used the ice axe.' 'What're you talking about? Adri's in a flap. She said you were acting weird, and that you said you weren't coming.' 'There were about ten of them, but we managed. You should've seen it.' 'Who's we? It's not funny, you dickhead. I'm all set to go here.' 'I've switched partners, Renan. I'm going to Bonete with my new friend here. I like him more than you. He doesn't talk much. I like people who don't talk much.' 'Come again? What new friend, you fuck-wit? Are you drunk? I hope you're not serious about not going –' 'I've been to Bonete and back already. It's no big deal. Go check it out if you want, but you'll get there second. Second-place winner is loser number one, isn't he?' '…' 'Anyway, I'm going to the hospital to get my forehead stitched up. Talk later. Take care.' 'What the fuck, you –' He hung up and glanced at the boy, who pretended he hadn't heard a thing. 'Want me to call your parents or someone? We're going to the emergency room at Mãe de Deus.' 'No.' 'But your parents –' 'No! Seriously, you don't need to call anyone. OK?' 'Can I ask why?' 'Because you can't. Can I get out? Stop the car. I want to get out.' The boy felt for the door handle. 'It's OK, it's OK. I just thought . . . forget it, I'll take responsibility for you. Relax.' The boy pulled the T-shirt away from his face and stared at him with an almost defiant expression, assessing whether or not he could trust him. He returned the look with intensity and felt like he was staring at himself fifteen years earlier. It was as if the boy were a version of himself who had reacted differently to a certain episode that he did everything in his power not to remember, but did, in quick flashbacks. He was the boy he'd have become if he'd confronted Uruguay and his gang late that night. His memories of what had happened near the clearing had been buried for fifteen years and now, as they resurfaced, they sent a shiver through him. The boy was the first to look away. He pressed the bloody T-shirt to his face again and leaned against the car door, hunched over in the seat, drops of blood and sweat sliding down his chest. He looked back at the street in front of him. He couldn't remember half of the drive to where he was now, on Padre Cacique Avenue. He put his foot down, seventy, almost eighty miles an hour, ignoring the electronic speed bump in front of Beira-Rio Stadium. His heroic fantasy was fading, but his image of himself in reality didn't fill the empty spaces left by the fantasy. He was neither the hero of his imagination nor the doctor. He glanced in the rear-view mirror and didn't recognize himself. Only the blood running down his forehead was incontestable, doing what blood does, beautiful and predictable. He turned right on José de Alencar, drove around the central reservation and pulled up at the emergency entrance to Mãe de Deus Hospital. He was careful to park so that he wouldn't obstruct the flow of other vehicles. A receptionist called a nurse and a doctor. He lied, saying a bunch of drunks had attacked them out of nowhere on a street in the southern suburbs. The boy was whisked off to emergency while he filled out the admittance forms, pressing an improvised bandage to his own forehead. Then he was also taken inside, but not to the same ward. They cleaned the wounds on his ear, neck and forehead. He didn't tell the doctor that he was a doctor himself. When they went to give him a local anaesthetic before stitching up the deep cut in his forehead, he asked them to do it without it. The doctor on duty insisted, saying it would hurt. Only then did he reveal that he was a doctor, to convince him that he knew exactly what to expect. After a brief discussion, the doctor agreed to suture him without the anaesthetic. It was very painful, but every time the needle pierced his flesh he was certain it was precisely what he had hoped to feel. It was a therapy of sorts, slowly soothing him, bringing his entire body back under control. Fifteen minutes later, with an enormous bandage of white gauze on his forehead, he looked for the ward where the boy was being treated. He found him on a bed with a drip in his arm. A doctor was suturing an ugly cut in his left eyebrow while two nurses were finishing cleaning his many wounds. He walked over and pressed the boy's nose lightly with his fingers. He moaned and the doctor turned to glare at him. He introduced himself and said the boy was his friend. 'Your nose must be broken.' 'That's what they said. They're going to take me for an X-ray soon. They reckon I've got some broken ribs too.' 'What's your name?' 'João.' 'João . . . Do you live over in Esplanada?' The boy didn't answer. 'Don't worry about anything, I've taken care of everything.' 'Thanks.' 'I'm going to write down my address and phone number on this piece of paper here, see. If you don't want them to call your parents or whoever, call me.' 'Thanks.' 'João . . . You know, I can't remember the real name of a single friend of mine from Esplanada. We all knew each other by nicknames.' 'Do you live in Esplanada?' 'Used to. Until a few years ago.' 'Thanks for helping me out there. Those guys were going to kill me, I guess.' 'I don't doubt it.' 'What was that thing you hacked them with?' The doctor and the two nurses stopped what they were doing for a fraction of a second then quickly went back to work. The boy grimaced, recognizing his slip, and asked, 'Where did you live in Esplanada?'

'507 Rodonel Guatimozim. The one with the exposed-brick walls.' 'I'm not sure which one that is.' 'So you live around there too?' 'Nearby.' 'I still know some guys that live there, I think. Pellet. The Joker, too.' 'Don't know him. The Joker . . .' The boy laughed at the nickname. The doctor finished suturing the wound and one of the nurses began to prepare a bandage. 'Funny thing is, only the guys had nicknames, the girls never did. We called them all by their names. Isabela, Ingrid . . .' 'I've got a friend called Isabela too, but it wouldn't be the same person. Course not, she's my age, duh.' 'Lara, Naiara . . .' 'I reckon Naiara still lives there.' 'Huh?' 'I think I know who she is. She still lives nearby.' 'Really?' 'Isn't she the one who runs a day-care centre?' 'Dunno. I haven't talked to her in years.' A nurse informed them that everything was ready for them to go to the X-ray room. 'Where does this Naiara live?' 'Hmm, I don't know the name of the street . . . I know it's kind of, like, on a corner, and she's got a day-care centre in her house, there are some children's pictures on the outside wall . . . near the hill . . .' The nurse looked at them impatiently, with a wheelchair ready. 'João, I have to go. I'll call the hospital later to see how you are.' He nodded.

THE CLEARING

No one could remember a winter that had arrived with such great force. From one day to the next, there was a thirty-five-degree drop in temperature and the wind chill that Friday night made it feel even colder than the forty-six degrees Fahrenheit predicted in the *Lunchtime News*, doing justice to the portentous expression 'polar air mass'. At Hermano's house, the fridge was powered down to the lowest setting, woollen quilts were brought down from the tops of wardrobes and placed at the foot of every bed, electric heaters were left in the bathrooms to make it easier to get out of the shower, and the aroma of his mother's onion soup, a tradition in the cold months, wafted into every room in the house. On his bike rides to and from school, in the early morning and right before lunch, the icy wind had sandpapered Hermano's face and now, in the afternoon, his skin was dry, sensitive and taut. People went about underdressed, many in flip-flops and T-shirts, surprised by the change of weather or still unable to assimilate the new temperature, hunched over and focused on their own discomfort.

Early in the afternoon, protected by tracksuit bottoms, a nylon jacket and a thick, striped wool scarf, Hermano walked to Walrus's house. The door to the new and bigger garage, with its shiny coat of brown paint, was ajar. Hermano rang the doorbell and heard Walrus shout for him to come in through the garage. He no longer had to fear the dogs, because a few days earlier Armageddon and Predator had bared their teeth and turned on Skinny Face, who had whisked out his revolver and put a bullet through their skulls. The garage was completely empty inside, with paw- and footprints in the layer of dust coating the dark-red flagstones. As he entered the house, Hermano noticed that cardboard boxes were scattered everywhere, most of them open, containing all manner of domestic objects thrown in at random. The shelves were empty and the furniture looked as if it had been dragged here and there. Hermano climbed the stairs to the second floor and went into Walrus's room. Bricky was already there. They hadn't waited for him to arrive to start playing *Stunts*. It was their favourite computer game, with simple but fluid 3D graphics, realistic physics, an enormous variety of cars, a replay function, and a tool that allowed you to create new racetracks with great freedom, placing curves, ramps, drawbridges, loop-the-loops, barriers, oil slicks, and even scenic elements such as trees and buildings, wherever you wanted. Every now and then the trio would get together at Walrus's house to create new tracks and then spend hours breaking records. When Hermano walked in, they were hunched over the monitor, adjusting the details of a new track. Without taking his eyes off the screen, Walrus said:

'Check it out. We're making a track that's impossible to finish.'

Hermano pulled up a stool. The atmosphere in the room was weird. In general, events on the monitor, whatever they were, were powerful enough to be their sole focus for hours and hours. This time, however, it was as if the game were only a pretext to divert their attention from other uncommonly weighty topics. Staring intently at the screen, they didn't need to look at one another. Discussing what kind of obstacle should be placed at the end of a series of loops, that early-winter day, they avoided talking about things that were changing their lives for ever.

About a week earlier, the shocking news that Bricky was going to be a father, at the age of fifteen, had spread through Esplanada. No one knew who the girl was. She lived in Tristeza, was sixteen, had never been seen with Bricky, and he had never spoken about her. After disappearing for a few days, Bricky came out, confirmed the rumours and announced that he was taking responsibility for the child. The two families had met and the situation would be dealt with. The information he gave was succinct and precise. His tone was that of a boy who had become a man and planned his entire future in a matter of two or three days. What his plans were, no one knew for sure. When the rumour reached Hermano, he found it hard to imagine his friend even having a sex life. Imagining him as a father was nothing less than absurd. Bricky was his best friend. They played video games and football together and liked to talk about the films they got for free from Bricky's parents' video rental shop. They were almost the same age and had grown up together. An active sex life must have seemed as unthinkable to Bricky as it did to Hermano. A child must have seemed as remote and implausible to Bricky as it did to Hermano. But now it was clear that things weren't what they seemed. Despite their friendship, or because of it, they couldn't talk about it. True intimacy appeared to depend on their ability to talk about what was going on in Bricky's life, but now they discovered they didn't know how to exchange confidences of that nature. There was no point talking about video games any more. There was no point parodying dubbed dialogue in *Escape from New York* or *Commando*. Inside jokes were losing their effect. Bricky was going to be a father. When they were five or six years old, the two of them had combed the thickly vegetated vacant plots of land in Esplanada for exotic ingredients with which to prepare imaginary elixirs, potions and poisons. Armed with bottles of perfume, small jam jars, knives, spoons, droppers, syringes and a spade, they had harvested leaves from weeds, evil-looking little red berries that grew on thorny bushes, roots, milky sap, insects, arachnids, moist soil taken from secret locations, water from puddles and murky ponds covered with green scum, a long list of ingredients that they measured and combined with rigorous attention, following previously invented recipes. There was a potion for hibernating all winter long, and others that bestowed superpowers such as the ability to talk to dogs, to move objects with the power of one's mind, like Luke Skywalker, and to not feel pain. The dark branch of their childish alchemy included poisons that could blind, take away a cat's ability to always land on its feet, and, the most important one of all, the most secret and powerful recipe: a liquid that would instantly kill a girl if sprinkled on her skin. It was a mixture of gutter water, pieces of a white flower that grew in the front garden of the ugly boy who would later

come to be known as the Joker, an orange fungus
that grew on rotten tree trunks, spider legs and,
finally, the most coveted and dangerous ingredient
of all: a live yellow wasp. They kept an ample stock
of the nefarious mixture hidden in a buried box.
When and why they might need to kill a girl didn't
even occur to them. But they were certain the
potion was of vital importance. Until proven otherwise, all girls were threats and to be regarded with
suspicion. The secret recipe was a defence that
united the boys against *them*. When he heard his
friend confirm the rumour about the pregnancy,
Hermano remembered the poison they'd made as
children. The secret stock was probably still there,
but neither of them could have remembered exactly
where it was buried. Somewhere in his subcon-
scious, in spite of having recently got to know
Bonobo's sister a little better, there were still traces
of the conviction that girls were to be fought, not
made pregnant. Hermano felt betrayed. He recognized the irrationality of the feeling, but he also
knew that reason had no power over certain emotions, and so he let the feeling be, without trying
to suppress it. It wouldn't be long, he was sure,
before he felt happy for his friend.

Wallace Wissler, for his part, was about to move
somewhere yet to be determined. His explanations
were vague because he really didn't know much,

but his dad, Skinny Face, was in trouble with the police. The move would be quick, that weekend. This was the last time they'd play computer games at his place. It was also possibly the last time they'd ever see him, but no one dared say it out loud. He wouldn't be missed by most people, but Hermano and Bricky had a bond with him – a bond that was less about pity than they cared to believe. Wallace still didn't know if he was going to live with his mother in the state of Santa Catarina or with his father God knows where.

Although he felt abandoned, Hermano's betrayal was perhaps the worst of all, because it had nothing to do with an accident, a twist of fate or any other factor outside his control. On the one hand, he was spending more and more time alone, locked in the house or immersed in his crazy routine of bike rides, runs and solitary exercise. On the other hand, he was spending less time in the company of his childhood friends to spend more time with Bonobo. You couldn't say that he and Bonobo were close, but even their occasional encounters seemed to demand all of Hermano's energy for sociability. There were also the rumours that Hermano and Naiara were a couple, or at least going out occasionally. It wasn't true. He did everything he could to avoid Naiara in public. He'd leave the minute she showed up anywhere, or, if that wasn't possible, he'd find a way not to exchange a word with her. Nevertheless, it was true, he'd gone back to Bonobo's place on a few occasions to spend time with her. They'd never gone beyond confessional conversations that culminated in kissing and groping each other. The memory of what had happened the first time they'd been alone together loomed in his mind as something both good and bad, success and failure, victory and frustration, a succession of moments recorded in vivid imagery, but which always came back to him accompanied by a disturbing feeling that he couldn't put his finger on.

The computer game distracted them from the awareness that from then on everything was going to be drastically different. They managed, for a few hours, to build and test a track that couldn't be finished. The sequences of obstacles were so difficult that it was impossible to accelerate the car enough to make it through certain loopings and jump from one side of a drawbridge to another. They spent as long testing the track with every possible car model as they'd spent creating it. Even the Formula One car, a champion at acceleration and final speed, ended up totalled. Convinced that it was 100 per cent impossible to get to the home stretch, they decided they were satisfied with their work and said goodbye. Hermano and Bricky left, while

Walrus began disconnecting cables in order to dis-assemble the computer.

The night sky was clear and in the direction of the Guaíba an almost imperceptible incandescence could be seen, a red vestige of dusk like a door closing behind the night. There was something solemn in the air, and the whole neighbourhood was heading home for a long period of waiting out the cold. They walked side by side for three blocks, cursing the weather, and parted ways with a firm handshake after a brief moment of eye contact. Hermano walked the last few blocks to his house quickly, feeling his sweat cooling beneath his T-shirt and nylon jacket.

The smell of soup evoked afternoons of TV-watching, lying on the sofa, rolled up in blankets. His parents were sitting at the kitchen table, his mother already mopping up the last drops of soup in her bowl with tiny chunks of bread, his father sucking down spoonfuls with his chin cautiously projected over the steaming bowl, yellow broth dripping from his spoon. Hermano got himself a bowl from the back of the cupboard, ladled in some soup and sat down. His father wiped his moustache with a napkin and asked how things were going. Hermano assured him that everything was fine. His mother got up, left the kitchen and came back holding a green report card. She handed it to his father, who left his spoon in the bowl, opened the report card, studied it for a moment, then looked at Hermano with a wry smile. He asked what was going on in a tone that was reassuring. His father was a serious man who rarely raised his voice. He had a square face, and Hermano had inherited his broad shoulders and arms too long for his torso. His father had worked for many years as the manager of a local food distributor, read the *Zero Hora*, *Folha de São Paulo* and *O Globo* religiously in two daily shifts, at breakfast and after dinner, and played doubles tennis with three old friends on Wednesday nights and Saturday mornings at the Professor Gaúcho Club. Hermano said there was no problem. For the first time in his life, he'd flunked two subjects, Portuguese and History, and would have to sit the tests again. He'd scraped through in his other subjects. He wasn't a brilliant student, but he'd never had to try very hard to pass. He studied little, on the eve of exams, in short bursts that never exceeded half an hour. It wasn't difficult. But that term he'd simply forgotten to study. He'd attended class on automatic pilot; it was all completely meaningless. There was no reason. There was no problem. He'd pay more attention, go through his notes and textbooks again before the tests. His father wasn't too pleased with the nonchalance of his reaction. School had never been a problem before, and it shouldn't become one at this stage in the game. Hermano swallowed a spoonful of soup and nodded. His father went off to read *O Globo* in front of the television. His mother sat beside him and they smoked their once-a-day cigarettes, he, Camel, she, Carlton, a decade-long habit. Hermano showered, set the alarm on his clock radio for 11 p.m. and fell asleep.

He awoke at eleven, pulled on a pair of jeans and a wool-lined jacket, told his mother, who was still in front of the TV, that he was going out to meet some friends, and headed for the clearing. He crossed the square and walked through unlit streets, moving further away from the centre of the neighbourhood, where there was a greater concentration of homes, towards more deserted blocks that were yet to be built on. On the pavement of the last street, City Council employees working on the electrical grid had dug a number of holes for lamp posts, but hadn't had time to finish. A few concrete lamp posts were lying in a large vacant plot of land, vaguely lit by a bright half-moon. Flanking the pavement on the right-hand side of the street was the Jungle, a black forest agitated by the chirring of crickets and the scandalous yowls of stray cats mating. At the spot marked by a rusty paint can hanging from a branch, Hermano disappeared into the trees.

Most of the children in Esplanada could walk the

hundred-yard trail with their eyes closed, though only the older ones went there at night and had their parents' permission to do so. He reached the clearing just as Bonobo threw a jar of petrol on a pile of dry branches, transforming the shy flame into a thundering bonfire. He saw Chrome Black, the Joker and Isabela. He also recognized Livramento and Savage, two of Bonobo's friends who, it was said, were responsible for more than one house burglary in the region. There was another guy and a girl Hermano didn't know. As expected, no sign of Naiara. She and her brother didn't usually mix.

A gallon bottle of sweet red wine was being served in plastic cups which Hermano had to re-refuse every five minutes. Bonobo lit a cigarette in the fire and told them about an accident he'd seen on Serraria Road the previous Sunday that had been given a quarter of a page in the *Zero Hora*. An employee of a motorbike repair shop in Ipanema had thought it'd be harmless to take a client's Kawasaki Ninja 1100 for a spin that sunny afternoon. He was doing about ninety-five miles an hour, according to a police estimate, when he was surprised by a horse and cart emerging from a side street to cross the road. The employee wasn't wearing a helmet, and his head had collided with the horse's. The Kawasaki Ninja had gone flying in one direction and the employee in the other. The employee had hit his head again mid-flight, this time against a wooden post. The result, a few seconds later, was a dead body in a pool of blood, pink bits of brain stuck to the post, a Kawasaki Ninja transformed into a compact ball of twisted metal, a dead horse lying on the ground with its head facing the wrong way, a capsized cart, and a cart driver with an exposed fracture in his arm. The conversation stayed on the topic of car accidents and then broadened out to include stories of all kinds of accidents. At the age of twelve the Joker had lost his balance on a rock at a beach in Santa Catarina and fallen into the choppy sea. He'd been rescued, covered in lacerations, by two surfers. Isabela had fallen on some glass and had had twenty-two stitches in her shin. Hermano told some stories of falls from his bike. Time passed and soon everyone but him was drunk. They had finished the bottle of wine quickly and it was suggested that someone go get another bottle at the Maragato, a bar that stayed open well after midnight. Hermano volunteered, and Bonobo said he'd go with him to buy cigarettes.

They walked for about twenty minutes. At the Maragato, Bonobo went behind the counter and disappeared through a door with the owner of the bar. On the way back, he showed a little brick of marijuana to Hermano, who remained firm in his resolve to abstain for life from any and all substances that might be bad for him, which didn't stop him from feeling excited by the simple fact of having accompanied Bonobo on such an expedition. Hermano had earned his trust. The gallon bottle was heavy, but he insisted he could carry it on his own.

Shortly before they reached the paint can marking the trail to the clearing, Hermano spotted some silhouettes in the vacant plot of land on their left and recognized Uruguay's compact body and long hair well before Bonobo, who kept walking quickly with his head down for a few seconds before he realized they weren't alone. The word came out of Bonobo's mouth with a strange serenity, as if he had carefully placed it in the air:

'Run.'

For a split second Hermano was confused. Run, why? Oh, yes, that was obvious. But where? Towards them? Back to the Maragato? Into the forest? Before he knew it, Bonobo was already charging across the cobblestones towards the clearing, where the others were sitting around the fire, waiting for the wine. Hermano dropped the bottle in the middle of the street and ran too. That was something he was good at. Running. He caught up with Bonobo with ease and looked over his shoulder. There were five or six of them and at least two were holding objects that looked like pieces of wood or iron bars. A brick shattered some six feet to his left. He was relieved they were running. Fleeing like this was something he'd never have associated with Bonobo, him of all people: the invincible Bonobo, the toughest kid not only in Esplanada, but in all the southern suburbs, a fame that had spread to surrounding areas. He'd beaten up eight guys at the same time and had given a guy who'd threatened him with a revolver a serious working-over. There were dozens of infamous stories, but now Bonobo was running and Hermano was glad. The very thought of a confrontation came accompanied by flashes of terror that urged him to run even faster. He saw the first holes left by the City Council in the pavement, and further along he saw the lamp posts lying on the ground and knew now that they were only two blocks away from the trail to the clearing. If they made it there, the others would help defend them. Hermano ran as fast as he could and began to pull ahead of Bonobo. Then he heard a cry, followed by the plea:

'Shit, gimme a hand!'

He looked over his shoulder and couldn't understand where Bonobo was. All he could see was Uruguay and the others running down the middle of the street, still at a safe distance.

Where was Bonobo?

Uruguay kicked something on the ground. From the dull thud, he could tell it wasn't a rock or a can.

The thing didn't move, because soon the others started taking swings at it too.

Hermano dashed for the trees, tumbled in a ditch and hid behind leaves and branches. He couldn't see much of what was going on in the street, but he could hear it perfectly well. No one shouted, no one spoke. There was just the sound of trainers continuously kicking what could only be Bonobo for what felt like an hour.

But the hour ended and Hermano's heart was still thumping like mad. He tried to control his breathing, but it was impossible. They stopped kicking and began to talk. They appeared to be arguing. He made out a few curse words and little else. 'Shake him,' someone said. Thinking they'd come for him next, he listened hard for his name, but Uruguay and company sprinted off. They'd let him off. He heard the sound of their footsteps fading away until they disappeared. He stayed there, squatting behind the branches for a few minutes, waiting for Bonobo to make a sound. Nothing.

Before explaining why his face was covered in blood, after dashing breathlessly into the clearing where everyone was still sitting around the fire waiting for the gallon of wine, he took a few moments to register the look of surprise on each of their faces, revelling in the expressions that conveyed their certainty that he, Hermano, had just taken part in a violent episode, a conflict from which only he had escaped and returned to warn the others, bearing on his face the marks of an unquestionably real fight, and it was only after some insistence and probing about what had happened and where the hell Bonobo was that he began to relay the events of the last few minutes, starting with the moment he and Bonobo had been surprised by Uruguay and his rabid gang and they had dashed for the clearing, hoping the others would be able to help them in a fight that wasn't going to be easy, as there'd been six or seven of them, armed with bricks and pieces of wood, until something unbelievable had happened: Bonobo had been supremely unlucky and fallen into one of the holes that the fucking council workers had dug for the lamp posts on the Friday afternoon, which the cunts hadn't bothered to fill in or fence off, probably because they were in too much of a hurry to start the weekend with a cachaça in some shithole of a bar, and Bonobo had ended up falling into one and getting stuck, with one arm pinned inside and the other sticking out, scrabbling at the earth and plants around him in a futile attempt to free himself, and as soon as he'd realized Bonobo wasn't with him, Hermano had stopped, looked back and seen that Uruguay and company were kicking Bonobo's unprotected head, which was the only exposed part of his body except for his arm, battering him cruelly, and Hermano had had no choice but to go back and try to pull the bastards off him, and he'd even tried to reason with them, to get them to stop that cowardly attack, but they weren't in the mood for chit-chat and not only had they continued to kick Bonobo but they'd also come after Hermano, who'd done his best to defend himself and try to save his friend at the same time, but all he'd managed to do was get himself punched in the face, knocked to the ground and kicked relentlessly, like Bonobo's head, until they'd grown tired and left, laughing and saying who's the tough guy now, hey, hey, unconcerned by the fact that Bonobo was motionless, his head hanging to one side, apparently unconscious, the only difference being that people who are unconscious breathe and, from what Hermano had seen, horrified, Bonobo wasn't breathing, his face was smashed in and inert and he didn't respond when he called his name and slapped him and shook him, and when he'd felt his friend's neck and wrist for a pulse he hadn't been able to find one, and he'd freaked out and come running to get the others, who barely waited for Hermano to finish his story and charged down the trail through the dark forest to find Bonobo in the hole in the pavement, all except Hermano, who stayed squatting by the fire a moment as he recovered his composure, going over every detail of the story he'd just told and memorizing the things he'd changed or omitted, because the truth was he hadn't gone back to help Bonobo, he'd remained crouched in the forest like a coward while an assault took place only a few feet away, an assault whose details he'd only discovered a few minutes later, when he plucked up the courage to venture into the street and found Bonobo in the hole, with an arm and his head sticking out, dripping with blood, even from his ears, blood devoid of beauty, which reminded him more of roadkill, unbreathing, with that absence of organic vibration that could only mean he was lifeless – it was death, and a death in which Hermano instantly felt implicated, as a result of his cowardice, which had finally emerged in its entirety and which he was determined to keep secret, for he wouldn't be able to go on living if he had to wear it like a brand on his forehead for the rest of eternity, if he had to be the gutless wonder who'd sneaked into the forest without a sound while a gang had beaten his friend to death; no, that would have been unbearable, and the solution he'd found at the time had come in the form of a blow – not a figure of speech, but a literal blow that Hermano had delivered to himself, punching himself in the face, after which he'd thrown himself to the ground and rolled in the dirt and tugged at his T-shirt until it tore, and punched himself again, over and over, and finally discovered what it felt like to take and throw punches in a real fight, a series of sharp, throbbing pains that brought to mind the shapes of bones and the arrangement of facial nerves, that grew until they became a single pain, not as sharp but more all-encompassing, duller, easier to bear with each new blow, the taste of his blood, somewhat sweet and sour, like tart tomato sauce, surging readily from his split lip, his nose, a cut in his eyebrow, and after the first few minutes of pain the whole thing had actually become easy; it had been a relief to finally feel it for real, to feel it in his own flesh for the first time rather than in wild daydreams, movies and comic books, to let it happen for the first time and discover that feeling it was easy, imagining it was hard.

8.04 A.M.

It took almost twenty minutes to get back to Esplanada in the morning heat. The Montero seemed to float over the tarmac, as if carried by a calm, swift-flowing river. The warm breeze came through the broken windshield. The twenty-minute drive felt as if it had taken thirty seconds as he turned right on to Serraria Road, once again entering that territory which, seen from above, might have comprised a kind of open map of his life, with captions for everything he'd felt and experienced in thirty years of existence, a neighbourhood which had once been the cosmos and was now a toy town that he drove through, stirring up old ghosts. The old stairs where they used to hold downhill races were still there, except that they looked about a third of the length and had been redone, with regular granite steps, green steel railings, and beds of daisies on both sides, replacing the hard dirt of times past. He parked at the top of the stairs, got out and sat on the first step. On his left was Police Hill, still intact and uninhabited due to its restricted

access. On his right he saw the still-serene Guaíba
River and Ipanema Beach, in a state of meditation
before the tumult and noise of the Sunday afternoon, which would reverberate with bass notes
from car sound systems and the nervous drone of
jet skis. At eight o'clock in the morning, however,
the relative silence was still sovereign, echoing the
silence of that long-ago night when he and Bonobo
had sat in that very spot, as they returned home on
foot from a party. So many years later, he could
still remember the feeling of wanting to be like
Bonobo: awe-inspiring, tough, spontaneous – and
respected, despite being ugly, uncouth, brutal, and
at odds with the world. To spend time with him
was to flirt with a world radically different from
the inner world of his adolescence, and, for a short
time, marked by their exchange that night at the top
of the stairs, it had seemed possible to reconcile the
two worlds, to belong to one but participate in the
other often and with such confidence that life would
expand beyond who he was, cheating boundaries
in a promiscuous mingling of personalities, tem-
peraments and outlooks. He had tried to get close
to Bonobo in order to feel comfortable in his own
skin, and it had worked. Not for long, but it had
worked. Until the tragedy had taken place and the
truth had imposed itself: he would never be anyone
but himself, and to insist on being someone else

was a waste of energy, not to mention a source of frustration, shame and regret. So many times in the intervening years he had stopped whatever he was doing to find a quiet corner, hunch his shoulders, clench his fists, punch walls and sometimes even shed a tear or two, wishing he could turn back time and defend Bonobo from being beaten to death, even if it meant getting himself killed, because it was the right thing to do, it was what the man he wished he was would have done in that situation, regardless of the consequences. There was nothing heroic about living, however. At thirty, life felt like an endless rehearsal for a heroic moment that never arrived. A permanent limbo between innocence and heroism, inhabited by ghostly projections of himself, distorted by what he wished he had been or wanted to become. He ran his eyes over the houses on the slope in front of him to the place where the neighbourhood levelled out. He tried to remember what Bonobo had said, where he'd pointed that night in the hours they'd spent at the top of the stairs. The plot of land was near Police Hill. There was a water tank. The old points of reference, such as trees and lamp posts, were useless in the new urban density. Off in the distance, he spied the water tank, the street corner, a colourful wall, and remembered what the boy had said at the hospital, about the day-care centre, the pictures on the wall. He assessed the distance, visualizing the streets he'd have to take to get there, then stood so quickly he almost lost his balance, and got in the car. He drove for a few minutes until he found the wall decorated with clumsy paintings of cartoon characters. That was where Bonobo would have built his house one day, if he'd lived long enough to work and save a little money, instead of being murdered semi-accidentally in Uruguay and his gang's vindictive rampage. He parked, got out, and clapped his hands since there was no doorbell. It was early for a Sunday; no one answered. He clapped again. There was a closed iron gate set into the wall and a ten-foot path up to the front door. Next to the house, partially hidden from view, was a canvas swimming pool for children, a plastic slide and some scattered toys. He shook the gate, but it didn't make much noise. He clapped for the third time and the front door opened. Naiara was about six inches taller. Her face was bonier, her nose pointier, her eyes deeper set. The dyed-red hair was the most striking difference between her and the image of the slender thirteen-year-old that was still branded in his memory. He, in turn, knew that he was almost identical to his fifteen-year-old self, not only physically, but in everything, which was why she recognized him immediately, not without some surprise in her eyes.

'For some reason, I knew I'd see you again one day.' 'Hi, Naiara.' 'The guy who used to climb the stairs three at a time.' She was wearing a loose-fitting blue blouse with white lace trim and a long white skirt. He couldn't tell if she'd been woken by his clapping or if she was already up. She reached back into the house for a key ring and a packet of cigarettes. She pulled out a lighter and lit up. 'Horse Hands. Exam Man.' 'My God, no one's called me that in a long time.' 'First place in medicine at the Federal.' 'Horse Hands, that is.' 'What did you do to your forehead?' 'I got in a fight with about ten guys. You should have seen what I did to *them*.' She laughed as they had so many years earlier, he, Bricky and their other friends, when they did voiceovers for everyday situations with lines from dubbed action movies. 'Still falling off your bike, hey?' she said, coming over to the gate. She selected one of the keys from the half-dozen on the plump, heart-shaped key ring, made out of some kind of red foam, and unlocked the gate. He stepped through. They sat facing one another at the kitchen table and drank bitter black coffee that Naiara reheated in a metal coffee pot. She must have been twenty-eight, he figured. They exchanged quick synopses of their lives, as old acquaintances do. She smoked a cigarette every ten minutes, letting the smoke waft aimlessly from her mouth and nose as she spoke. She hadn't been able to have children of her own and had lived with two different men, but now she was on her own, sharing the house with a cousin who was also single. They both worked in the day-care centre next to the house. He told her he'd been married for five years, was a plastic surgeon and had a two-and-a-half-year-old daughter named Nara. 'Nara?' she asked with a wistful smile. He remembered a series of moments they'd shared, so long ago now, but enough to feel that they still had a special connection, theirs alone, in memories that were still retrievable, although they no longer had much bearing on the present. The cousin wandered into the kitchen in a nightgown. She apologized, Naiara introduced them, and the cousin left through the same door, saying she was going to put on something decent. They sat in silence for a time, not sure what else to say. Naiara filled a kettle with water and put it on to boil. The window was open and the sun was already blazing outside. She asked if he drank *chimarrão*, but he didn't answer. He stood. It was time to go.

THE FUNERAL

Esplanada was finally becoming a community. Within the imaginary boundaries that separated that set of streets from the rest of the city, the sons and daughters of the oldest residents had become couples, and some had married. Some of these had stayed on in the neighbourhood, taking out mortgages and having children of their own. Litters of cats and dogs had been shared among the locals, making the pet population increasingly dense and contributing to the frenzied barking that broke out at random late at night. There was a constant exchange of fresh spices, fruit and vegetables from private gardens, as well as seedlings, tools, construction materials, books, records, videotapes and every imaginable favour that a good neighbour could possibly do another: lifts to school, invitations to barbecues, exterminating snakes and spiders, and feeding dogs while the owners were away on vacation. Successive generations of childhood friends had grown up together, forming bonds that they sometimes believed would last for ever, each new phase of life resembling the last. There was pride and an authentic neighbourhood provincialism. What had been missing, and no one had noticed it before now, was tragedy. More specifically, a tragic death. And the fact that the first tragic death was that of Esplanada's most disliked resident, the embodiment of delinquency and gratuitous aggression in a relatively peaceful part of town, only fuelled, to the perplexity of all, feelings of abandonment, insecurity and distress, which ended up irreversibly unifying that group of individuals who, more by chance than anything else, had settled next to one another.

Hermano was aware of this process when sobbing broke out at the sight of the coffin being carried into the parlour where the wake was to begin. They were all there that cold Sunday morning. Bricky, Pellet, Walrus, Mononucleosis, the Joker, Chrome Black, Isabela, Ingrid, and a lot of people that Hermano didn't know very well but recognized as fellow residents. Entire families who had helped spread the bad news on the Saturday and had risen early on the Sunday, anxious to begin an initiation rite, pull on sober clothing and make their way to João XXIII Cemetery for the funeral of the young thug who had met with extraordinary violence at the hands of a gang that included another resident's son – who had stolen his father's motorbike that Friday night and was still on the run. Hermano's parents had taken him to the emergency room, where he was given two stitches in his left eyebrow and another in his lower lip. After repeating the story three or four times, he'd locked himself in his room on Saturday morning. It was his father who told his story to Bonobo's parents. On Saturday afternoon, he gave a statement to the police. Chrome Black, who knew Uruguay better, said he'd been talking for several days about teaching Bonobo a lesson because of the fight that had brought Isabela's fifteenth birthday party to an end. No one could say for sure who the other members of the gang were.

After Bonobo's family had completed the agonizing first cycle of bidding the body goodbye, few dared set foot in the parlour. Those who did went in alone. Bricky was one of the first. Hermano watched him from a distance to see what his reaction would be when he saw the body. Nothing. His face was unflinching as he stared at the corpse, and he left looking pensive. Hermano continued to watch his friend and saw him put his arm around a girl with red hair and very white, freckled skin. She was wearing a long skirt and a cropped jacket, both black, with a bright-red top under the jacket. He went over and congratulated them on the pregnancy. She smiled, and Bricky made a strange face, pressing his lips together and lowering his head a little, a mixture of disconcerted thanks and farewell, as if they were never going to see each other again.

Hanging in the air was a feeling shared by everyone, that few of them had had a chance to really get to know Bonobo. There were glimmers of regret when people looked at one another, perhaps a sense of guilt about having scorned, hated or feared that insolent, ugly youth who liked to beat people up and did it well. It was a feeling shared by Hermano. He knew, if he was honest with himself, that he hadn't established a deep bond with Bonobo in those last few months and that his absence would be easily forgotten. What most moved Hermano now were the tears of some of Bonobo's real friends. This sight made a tremendous impact. In front of him, Isabela leaned on Walrus's shoulder, tired of holding back her tears, and he put his arm around her awkwardly. It was the only moment in which Hermano thought he wouldn't be able to control the knot in his own throat. But he did.

Bonobo's parents were named Emiliano and Marta. He was over sixty, while she couldn't have been more than forty. They were sitting in the parlour, surrounded by a small group of relatives. Naiara was sitting on a bench, staring at her brother's coffin. She was accompanied by two friends, who stroked her hair and whispered words of comfort and encouragement. He'd have to face them sooner or later, so he took a deep breath and entered the parlour, lit by candles and weak yellow light bulbs. Emiliano stood to shake his hand and accept his condolences. He looked like a tired man who drank more than he should and had been married three or four times. He was wearing a faded wool cap that emphasized his sickly appearance, but his handshake was vigorous and his posture firm. Naiara had once told Hermano that her father owned a small printer's shop in the city centre where he produced stickers, notebooks and flyers. No matter how sick or alcoholic he looked, and Hermano wasn't sure of either, he was a guy who would live to be at least ninety. His only words were disconcerting:

'We're glad you're OK.'

Then he sat down again beside his wife, who was numb and a little out of orbit but thanked Hermano for coming and said she'd really like it if he paid them a visit in a few days' time so that they could talk, maybe in the afternoon, for coffee and a snack.

A shocking, unbelievable idea occurred to Hermano: Bonobo's parents saw him as a good influence on their son. If they knew what had really happened, they wouldn't be treating him like that. It was comical, in a way.

'What're you laughing at?'

The frail, lovely Naiara was staring at him with eyes slightly red from crying. Her thin little face looked even leaner, her cold-chapped lips contracted into almost nothing.

'Dunno.'

Hermano pulled her to him and hugged her as hard as he could, praying that in so doing he could let her know all the affection he felt for her and, at the same time, communicate his rejection. She sank her head into his neck as if she were immersing it in the water of a pool, holding her breath. Maybe if she were a little older, or prettier. He was always thinking about strong older women, as strong and mature as he felt himself to be. Naiara seemed so fragile. He couldn't look at her now. Slowly releasing the hug, seeing Naiara leave with short backward steps and a confused smile, he knew for certain that it was to be a day of final decisions. He just needed to concentrate a little and be alone somewhere. Before that, however, there was one last thing that had to be done at the wake: look at Bonobo's lifeless face.

His bones turned to jelly when he approached the coffin. The spray of flowers resting on the lid seemed like a provocation, designed to impress a contrast of life on the retinas of those who dared glance into the hole beside it. Bonobo's face was

probably covered. If memory served him, not much
of it had been left intact. It had to be covered. He
took a step forward and looked. The icy tremor
lasted a few seconds, but he quickly recomposed
himself. What he saw was a wax sculpture that
looked more artificial than dead. Bonobo's face was
exposed, clearly reconstructed, prepared and made
up. The cause of death had been cranial trauma.
He remembered that he had already seen Bonobo
dead, in fact, that night in the street. The image he
had approached then, with short, terrified steps,
was much grislier than this one, adapted for the
ritual. But while that one had been uglier, this one
was sadder and emphasized the absence of life even
more. He'd read in a comic book that Buddhists
believe that something of the person lingers in the
body for a while after death. It isn't easy to discon-
nect from the body. He didn't believe in souls, but
the Buddhist belief was in keeping with his impression that there was still something of Bonobo in
the hole that was no longer there at the wake. He
preferred to believe that what had been there
before, and which was now absent from the white,
subtly deformed face, was just blood. He concluded
that death was a body drained of blood, and left
the coffin.

Apparently, after seeing the body in the coffin,
he had, in the eyes of others, completed a phase

that freed him of some of the pain, making him available to be approached by people he knew and people he didn't who wanted to talk about the fatality, to hear details, names, or simply share a little silence. He needed to get out of there right away. He looked for his parents and almost ran to them when he saw them. He wanted to know what came next. The wake would last a while longer, then the body would be carried to the grave, which wouldn't be a hole in a grassy field but a kind of drawer or compartment, like the hundreds of others lining the many corridors of the high-rise cemetery. He told them he was going for a walk and that he'd meet them at the car a little later. He couldn't stand to be there any more.

He left the cemetery and walked quickly downhill towards Azenha. Everything was closed that morning and both cars and people were scarce. He eventually found a tavern that was open. Behind the counter was a man with an enormous moustache covering his lips, but there wasn't a customer in sight. A TV set high on the wall was showing Formula One. The red metal tables sponsored by a brand of beer were battered and rusty, but they were each covered with a pink-and-white-chequered tablecloth. Hermano sat at the first table, closest to the door. From the counter, the moustached bartender asked if he wanted to order something. Fanta.

He drank a little Fanta and sat there, waiting for his thoughts to take form. Minutes passed and nothing. No conclusion. His friends' lives were changing, and one had ended, but he was still there, with no conclusions. If he couldn't extract at least one little lesson from everything that was going on then he'd have to accept that life unfolded largely by chance and could be controlled only in its smaller details. And that couldn't be true. There were things he just knew, and this was one.

Naiara appeared in front of him.

'Your parents said you'd gone for a walk and I decided to try and find you.'

Hermano was annoyed. His meditation was being interrupted. He'd have to ignore her. He wouldn't be able to talk.

'Can I sit with you?'

He nodded. She sat. Silence. Then:

'Can I sit on your lap?'

No, the answer was no, but he suddenly changed his mind and saw that yes, of course she could sit on his lap, she had left her brother's wake to come and look for him, and she was right, why should they feel so alone just then?

'Sure.'

She sat on his thigh as modestly as it is possible to sit on someone's thigh, folded her arms across her chest and leaned her head on his shoulder. She was cold and her breaths were sighs. She was a young mammal. If he could have, he'd have loved her now. He waited a while to give deeper feelings a chance to manifest, to come to stay, but it didn't happen.

'Naiara, I'm not into you. I mean, not in a boyfriend–girlfriend kind of way. Sorry.'

'That's a shame, 'cause I'm into you.' She gave him a kiss on the cheek and retreated back into the position she'd been in. His leg was growing tired. 'Can I stay here anyway? For a little while?'

Without much intensity, he hugged her. It unsettled him more than death: wanting so badly to love someone and not being able to because it wasn't a choice. He felt that she was the only creature alive that really knew him, the only one who showed signs of understanding at least part of what was behind his scant words and actions. He wanted to fall in love with her, but couldn't. This incapacity intrigued him. While on the one hand it came with a feeling of impotence, on the other, by contrast, the kind of thing he wanted and *could get* was becoming clearer. He decided to concentrate on that, on the difference between the two things. He straightened his back and changed his position in the chair. He would leave only when he was filled with certainties.

Almost two hours later, he paid for the Fanta and

caught a bus home. Naiara had long since left. His parents had found him at the bar, but he'd turned down their offer of a lift and said he'd find his own way back. On the bus, he refined and simplified his plans. Now he knew exactly what to do. He wouldn't have to pretend any more.

ACKNOWLEDGEMENTS

The following people helped me to write this book with their patience, stories and/or critiques: Daniel Pellizzari, Mário Bortolotto, Nataniel Strack, Nelson Baretta, Pedro Jakobson, Rafael Braga and Tainá Müller. The novel Adri is reading in bed when she talks about the back-to-front musical chairs is *Millennium People* by J. G. Ballard. I shamelessly borrowed the expression from the Portuguese translation by Celso Nogueira.